"I Just Thoug Why I Left, Rorke."

"I don't want to know."

"But there were reasons…"

"I'm sure there were. But telling me isn't going to change anything. So why waste the time? If you'll excuse me, I have work to do." He turned back to the engine.

Callie's frustration gave her voice a sharp edge. "What happened to you? You were more compassionate at twenty…you were human, you had a heart. Now you're some kind of…of… heartless machine."

Rorke straightened to his full height. "What happened to me?" He laughed, a harsh, disbelieving laugh. "*You* happened to me."

Dear Reader:

Welcome to Silhouette Desire - provocative, compelling, contemporary love stories written by and for today's woman. These are stories to treasure.

Each and every Silhouette Desire is a wonderful romance in which the emotional and the sensual go hand in hand. When you open a Desire, you enter a whole new world - a world that has, naturally, a perfect hero just waiting to whisk you away! A Silhouette Desire can be light-hearted or serious, but it will always be satisfying.

We hope you enjoy this Desire today - and will go on to enjoy many more.

Please write to us:

Jane Nicholls
Silhouette Books
PO Box 236
Thornton Road
Croydon
Surrey
CR9 3RU

Hometown Wedding

PAMELA MACALUSO

First published in Great Britain in 1995 by Silhouette Books, Eton House, 18-24 Paradise Road, Richmond, Surrey TW9 1SR

© Pamela Macaluso 1994

Silhouette, Silhouette Desire and Colophon are Trade Marks of Harlequin Enterprises B.V.

ISBN 0 373 05897 7

22-9505

Made and printed in Great Britain

PAMELA MACALUSO

wanted to be a writer from the moment she realized people actually wrote the wonderful stories that were read to her. Since she is extremely curious and has an overactive imagination, writing is the perfect career for her. Curiosity is a necessary part of "research," and flights of fantasy can be called "plotting"—terms she prefers to "nosy" and "wool-gathering."

While she loves movies, Pamela would choose a good book over any other form of entertainment. It sometimes takes a search party to get her out of a library or bookstore.

For:
Joseph,
who gave up part of his garage.

Rob Smith,
whose time and talent
helped transform it into an office.

With special thanks to
Joe and Paul,
who kept the sawdust swept up.

One

Did she really want to do this now?

Calista Harrison knew she would be seeing Rorke O'Neil on this trip to Harrison, Vermont, since he was to be best man at Rachel and Steve's wedding, where she herself was to be maid of honor. There was no getting around the inevitable, but she could wait until they ran into each other, rather than following through on her plan to deliberately seek him out.

"No, get it over with so you can stop worrying," she said to herself. "That way, Rachel won't find out what an awkward position she has put you in by her and Steve's choice of wedding attendants."

She had accepted Rachel's invitation before she'd asked about the best man. After she knew, she hadn't had the heart to disappoint her friend by backing out.

But she didn't want any hostility between herself and Rorke interfering with the joy of the wedding events. Since Rorke was the injured party, it was up to her to make the first move and apologize.

Sticking with the decision she'd made before beginning the drive from New York City to Harrison, she turned her car into the driveway of O'Neil Automotive.

She spotted him immediately. He was in the service bay. Rorke. *Her* Rorke. No, just Rorke, she corrected. He had been hers once, but that was long ago. Ten years had gone by since she'd made her choice. Ten years... but it felt like yesterday.

Callie's senses of place and time were impaired, but her sense of sight was working overtime as she gazed out the windshield.

Six-foot-plus of powerful male casually leaned forward to look into the engine compartment of the car in front of him. Dark blue coveralls and black leather motorcycle boots—almost everything about him looked the same. He still wore his thick black hair too long to be called conservative and too short to be mistaken for a rock star.

Callie consciously took long deep breaths, trying in vain to slow her pulse rate. *Think of him as just another man. Pretend you're meeting him for the first time,* she instructed herself. Good advice, if only the rest of her body would cooperate with her brain.

All she needed was to use the icy self-control that had been instilled in her from an early age. The control that won her the admiration of friends and colleagues, the control that helped her deal with the toughest clients and most demanding managers at work and helped her keep more than one amorous male at bay.

The control she'd called on ten years ago to make the most difficult decision of her life and stick with it. Surely facing him today would be easier.

Slowly she got out of her car and walked into the service bay.

"Car trouble, Ms. Harrison?" Rorke asked, glancing up at her without changing positions. His voice was deep, but smooth—a familiar memory.

"No...no, I'd like to talk to you, if you have a moment?"

"So talk." He reached into his back pocket, pulled out a wrench and once again turned his attention to the car.

Over the years, she had imagined what it might be like to see him again—how they would look, what they would say to each other, whether there would be angry recriminations, a loving reunion or a bittersweet acknowledgment that everything had worked out for the best.

She'd pictured many possibilities, but none had come close to the stiff, formal role Rorke was playing.

It was clear he wasn't going to make this easy for her. "I came to apologize." She paused, but when there was no response from Rorke she continued. "For leaving Harrison without telling you." She caught her bottom lip between her teeth. *At least look at me,* she begged silently.

He stood up, set the wrench down and looked at her.

She had forgotten how blue his eyes were. Blue eyes glinting down at her—not a warm mischievous glint, but a cold glint—like sunlight reflecting off ice. Absolutely no sign of the love and tenderness she'd seen there once upon a time. His coldness made her wish his attention was still on the car.

"Don't give it another thought. I haven't."

"But I..." All the carefully thought out sentences explaining her reasons for what she'd done deserted her.

"Don't think I sat around brokenhearted after you left. Once I cleared the moonbeams out of my eyes, it was life as usual, sweetheart."

"I came to explain. Please let me explain, Rorke." She reached out her hand and set it gently on his arm. He was so warm, so hard, so real. She could feel the ripple of his muscles tensing and the roughness of his hair against her palm.

"Why? Why should I?" Rorke's voice broke through the sensual daze she'd fallen into. He looked down at her hand. Callie could see the muscles along his jawline tighten. Slowly she moved her hand away from him, and once again his gaze returned to her face. "Why should I listen to you? Let you ease your conscience?"

Ease her conscience? She'd wanted to ease the tension for Rachel's sake, but had she also hoped to ease some of her own hurt? Maybe so.

She wanted Rorke to understand why she'd left him; she wanted him to forgive her. The Rorke she had loved would have understood, would have forgiven, would have made the pain go away.

"I just thought you should know...."

"I don't want to know."

"But there were reasons...."

"I'm sure there were. But telling me isn't going to change anything. So why waste the time?" He picked up the wrench. "If you'll excuse me, I have work to do." He turned back to the engine.

Her frustration gave her voice a sharp edge. "What happened to you? You were more compassionate at twenty than you are now! You were human, you had a heart. Now you're some kind of...of...heartless machine."

Rorke straightened to his full height. "What happened to me?" He laughed, a harsh disbelieving laugh. "*You* happened to me."

Damn, he didn't need this!

Didn't he have enough to do holding up his end of Yankee Motorworks from his temporary office upstairs, getting the plant and his house ready, and filling in at the garage until his father could find another trained mechanic to replace the one who'd left town recently? He didn't have the time nor the energy to stroll down memory lane with Callie Harrison.

What difference did it make why she'd left him, why she'd changed her mind about marrying him, why she hadn't even bothered to say goodbye? He didn't want to know her reasons.

Over the years he'd speculated and theorized the situation from every possible angle. Again and again he came back to the words Chandler Harrison had thrown at him—Callie had gotten involved with him so she could bargain with her father.

When he and Callie had first become friends, she had told him about her father's insistence that she follow the family tradition of attending Harvard, then coming home and joining the family bank. Callie had wanted to study art. Her father had been appalled, but apparently Mr. Harrison thought art the lesser of two evils and agreed to finance her education at the college of her choice if she gave up Rorke.

She'd set a trap for him, and he'd walked into it. He'd been a fool to think the daughter of the richest man in town could truly be in love with the son of the local auto mechanic.

He was more than that now. For a moment he'd been tempted to tell her about Yankee Motorworks. Tell her what no one in Harrison knew yet. His father knew, but he hadn't told anyone. The elder O'Neil wasn't one to brag, and no one had asked.

Rorke had made a life for himself. After four years in the air force, Rorke had enrolled at MIT. Teaming up with a fellow engineering major and a business major, who'd shared his love of motorcycles, he'd cofounded Yankee Motorworks—a multimillion-dollar enterprise that continued to grow by leaps and bounds, its latest bound being their third plant, now under construction just outside Harrison.

Of course Rorke didn't blame the town for their lack of interest in his welfare—growing up he'd been called Harrison's one-man motorcycle gang.

When he'd moved back to Harrison last month, he'd decided to keep his connection to Yankee secret for a while. He didn't care one way or another who knew about his success and cared even less what they thought about it. But he knew that if his friend Steve had found out the house was Rorke's, he would have insisted on giving him a deal. Soon to be married,

Steve needed the extra money much more than Rorke did.

So Rorke and his friends bought the property for Yankee Motorworks. Although the plant was his pet project, Alex had represented Yankee at the ground breaking—as CEO. Rorke and Jesse dealt with the motorcycles, Alex dealt with how to sell them.

While Alex had never claimed the house was being built for him personally, the local paper and citizens of Harrison had assumed it was. Rorke saw no reason to tell them otherwise.

When he'd first left town, he'd vowed to make something of himself and show them all, but as the years went by and he joined forces with Alex and Jesse and they started Yankee, his focus shifted. He was working not to prove anything to anyone, but because he loved what he was doing.

He had to admit the one person he had most wanted to prove himself to had been Calista Harrison. He'd set out to show her that despite his humble beginnings he could rise up and be her social equal.

Callie.

He'd known she was coming to Harrison for the wedding, but forewarned hadn't been forearmed. Seeing her today he felt like he'd been sucker-punched.

She was still so damned beautiful—a beautiful golden-haired princess.

Once upon a time he'd given her his heart. Surprisingly, she'd taken it but she hadn't kept it. After playing with it, she'd thrown it back at him.

The wrench slipped, clattering as it fell. Rorke swore, spouting words he'd stopped using in anger years ago. He couldn't go on like this; he had two weeks and a wedding to get through. He didn't want any more stunts like she'd tried to pull on him today. He also didn't want the anger he felt to come to the attention of anyone else in town. Callie would be leaving in two weeks, but he would have to live with the consequences of any public outburst between them.

What they needed was a truce. He attacked the buttons on his coveralls.

And the sooner he got this taken care of, the better.

Fifteen minutes after leaving Rorke, Callie realized, in her haste to get away, she'd turned the wrong way out of the parking lot. Had it been a subconscious wish to go back to New York? To escape to the safe sterile world she'd built for herself?

She was numb. Rorke's anger had come as no surprise, but she had thought he would at least listen to her explanation. She had expected some bitterness, but not total hostility and refusal to hear her out.

When she'd left Harrison ten years ago, the vision of a brokenhearted Rorke had haunted her at first. The forlorn image had almost sent her running back several times despite her father's threats.

But she knew for Rorke's sake and his father's sake, she had to stay away from him. Her father was a powerful man and could easily have made good on his threats to ruin the O'Neils.

Leaving hurt her, too. She'd hurt even more when Rorke hadn't come after her.

To ease the pain, she'd managed to convince herself Rorke hadn't really loved her, that he'd moved on to someone else . . . that his proposal had been nothing more than pretty words whispered in the moonlight...that he'd used it as a ploy to get what he'd wanted from her...that he probably wouldn't have married her anyway.

After all, hadn't Grandmother Harrison warned her about "bad boys and scalawags who would say anything to trick innocent young girls into surrendering their virtue"?

This view of the situation had served her well until she'd returned to Harrison. Then the memories of Rorke had started coming to the surface.

She remembered the sight of him wheeling into town on his motorcycle and could almost hear Grandmother Harrison's voice saying, "He's nothing more than a cycle-driving scalawag. Of course, what can you expect? The way his mamma walked off and deserted him when he was seven years old..."

It had been the memory of the sad, little boy living with the stigma of his mother's desertion in a small town that had first driven Callie to offer friendship to the rebellious twenty-year-old he'd grown into. Her own mother had passed away when she was fourteen, so she knew the emptiness his loss must have made in his life.

Rorke hadn't been friends with any of the boys at Harrison High, and friendship didn't describe the relationship he had with the girls. Callie's soft heart had made her want to reach out to him. Initially, his worldliness, his wild reputation, and the sparks of awareness she felt around him had frightened her away. But she'd eventually overcome her reservations.

Meeting on back roads and in the woods outside Harrison, they'd built a friendship—a friendship that had developed into something more.

The full extent of the something more had been driven home today when she'd looked into his angry eyes. Now she knew for certain he'd meant every loving word he'd said to her—including his proposal of marriage.

The thought of marriage reminded her of Rachel's wedding. Her efforts to keep her personal life from affecting the festivities had accomplished nothing.

She would have to approach Rorke again. Not to explain, this time, but to get him to agree to keep the anger between the two of them and not let it interfere with the wedding. He wouldn't do it for her, but she felt certain he wouldn't want to do anything to jeopardize Rachel and Steve's happiness.

The conversation with Rorke played back through her mind. Something didn't add up.

He'd told her it had been business as usual for him after she'd left, but if he'd really put it behind him so quickly and didn't care, would he have lashed out, blaming her for his coldness?

For the first time, Callie stood apart from her own tangled emotions and looked back at the events of the past, putting herself in Rorke's shoes.

Pain kicked its way through her, pain so strong, she had to pull over to the side of the road.

She lowered her head until her forehead rested on the steering wheel, her eyes shut tight.

"My God, Callie, how could you have been so blind?" A tightness in her chest made each breath a struggle. "He opened up to you. He trusted you. He loved you. And how did you repay him? You drove off and deserted him . . . the same way his mother did!''

Her heart broke once again, this time for Rorke. For the wonderful, caring man she knew he was deep inside. The man she had helped him to discover. The man she had run away from.

She opened her car door, stumbled out and began to walk. Was it possible to walk fast enough to stay ahead of the shadow of self-loathing and disgust waiting to settle over her?

Ignoring the dampness of the roadside grass as it wet her sandaled feet, she pressed on. She had no idea how far she'd walked when a chain-link fence caught her attention. Walking the last few feet to the corner of the fence, she looked in. A sign proclaimed Under Construction For Yankee Motorworks.

The name sounded familiar, but she couldn't place it. It was possible she'd heard the name at work. The advertising agency she worked for handled many more clients than she was personally involved with. She wondered what the company made as she looked for clues through the fence.

The enclosed area had been cleared of trees and leveled. Several large concrete buildings stood in the center of the compound. Construction equipment and crews of men were busy working.

How she wished this were just another workday for her. As beautiful as the scenery outside the chain-link fence was, she would gladly trade it for the familiar sight of her easel, drafting table and computer.

She turned and started back the way she had come, her stride much slower than before. A pair of cardinals flew out of the nearby trees and darted across the road, drawing her attention to a large billboard.

Callie felt a pulse of energy race through her. Three motorcycles . . . red on the left, blue on the right and white in the middle and slightly ahead of the other two . . . each with a helmeted rider in matching leather standing next to it. The lettering above each bike identified the model: Yankee Spirit, Yankee Clipper and Yankee Pride.

The commercial artist in her admired the effective layout of the billboard, but her eyes were drawn again and again to the figure in the middle.

Something in the stance, the set of the shoulders, the way his arms were crossed over his chest, sent shivers racing through her. *Callie, you've watched too many movies if the sight of a guy in white can spark such a physical reaction.* The helmet visor was mirrored, preventing her from seeing his face. She couldn't help wondering what he looked like.

Shaking her head at the direction her mind had wandered, Callie continued walking. She hadn't had that kind of a physical reaction to a picture since she'd been a teenager drooling over the latest bubble-gum heartthrob.

The fantasy of the white knight riding to rescue the damsel in distress was more than likely the reason behind her reaction. The man's visored helmet was a modern version of the headgear wore by legendary knights in shining armor, and the situation with Rorke had definitely distressed this damsel.

At least the billboard had answered her question about Yankee Motorworks. The company made motorcycles. Harrison would certainly feel the effects of having a large plant nearby. The plant and the bill-board were quickly forgotten as once more she thought about Rorke and the two weeks ahead.

She was glad when she reached her car. The morning sun reflected brightly off the windshield as she opened the door and slid into the driver's seat.

"You shouldn't leave your car unlocked."

Two

Callie's breath caught in her throat, and her hands closed tightly around the steering wheel. She recognized the voice right away but was sure a stranger's voice would have created only slightly more turmoil within her. "I...I—you're probably right." Had Rorke decided to listen to her side of things, after all?

"I didn't mean to frighten you, but I think we need to talk."

Callie turned to face him. He had taken off the coveralls he'd been wearing earlier, revealing his usual well-worn blue jeans and pale blue work shirt, and he'd taken the time to wash his hands before coming after her.

"Rorke—" she started to say, but he held up his hand to stop her.

"I don't want to start where we left off at the garage. As far as I'm concerned, the past is history and I'd like to keep it that way. But we'll be seeing a lot of each other while you're here, and a truce for the duration would make things more comfortable for everyone."

It was what she had planned to ask for, but part of her longed to pour her heart out to him—to ask for his forgiveness, to melt the ice her youthful actions had unintentionally left around his heart. "A truce is a good idea. Rachel deserves a happy wedding."

Rorke looked thoughtful. "How much does Rachel know? Could she have set up this reunion as a matchmaking ploy?"

"No." Callie shook her head. "Rachel doesn't know that we were—"

"Lovers?" Rorke filled the short pause.

Suddenly the interior of the car felt much too small and intimate a space for them to be having this conversation. She was uncomfortably aware of the knowledge that she had seen and touched the warm male body occupying the seat next to her. "I was going to say friends," she said softly. "I thought we weren't going to discuss the past."

"We aren't, but I would like to know who knows what."

"Rachel doesn't know anything about any of it. And neither does anyone else. I've never told anyone anything." *Except her father.* And only then because he'd interrupted her packing, but she hadn't told him *everything.* All she'd admitted was that she loved Rorke and was going off to marry him.

Shifting in his seat to face her more fully, Rorke crossed his arms over his chest. "Didn't want to admit to slumming, Ms. Harrison?"

"No! No, that's not why," she denied. Ten years ago, when rumors were flying about the very proper, very polite Miss Harrison and that hellion O'Neil, Callie had laughed it off as a case of mistaken identity, not even confiding the truth to her best friend. The developing love between them had been so new, so special. She had clutched her feelings and emotions tightly to herself, sharing them only with Rorke.

"Are you going to tell Rachel?"

"No, there's no reason to. If I told her now, I'm sure she would feel guilty about pairing us up for the wedding and then probably start a matchmaking campaign to get us back together."

Rorke frowned. "Then, by all means, don't tell her."

Callie knew the last thing they needed was Rachel on a whirlwind matchmaking rampage, but hearing Rorke speak out against it rankled. "Have you told Steve anything?"

"No, I never told anyone, either. Although I guess I should warn you, when you didn't show up as we'd arranged, I did go up to your house looking for you."

"Did you see my father?"

"Yes. Didn't he tell you?"

"No." Didn't Rorke know she and her father weren't on speaking terms? She was sure the rest of the town knew. "Did he ask about the rumors? What did you tell him?" *And more importantly, what had her father told Rorke?*

"He had plenty of questions, but I didn't tell him anything. If he's told you otherwise, he's lying."

"I appreciate your telling me, and I'm sorry—"

"No, don't say anymore. I didn't tell you for your benefit. It serves my purposes to keep the facts buried."

Callie smiled coolly. "Of course, how stupid of me to think otherwise." *Don't you dare let him see that his words hurt you.*

"Now that we have that settled, I'd better get back to work," Rorke said.

If only he'd let her explain, he would realize the reason he had work to go back to was because she'd walked away from him. O'Neil Automotive might have ended up only a memory if she'd stayed.

Maybe that would break his cool facade. At least it made her feel better to realize she'd been able to give him that much—to have preserved the business his family had built over the years. "And I need to get to Rachel's. We've got a lot to do in the next two weeks."

Actually, she longed for him to stay and talk. The next time she saw him, they would probably be with Rachel and Steve. In fact, this might be the only time the two of them were completely alone together.

Rorke opened the car door and stepped out. He turned, leaning down to look in at her. "Don't forget we have a truce."

"No, I won't."

"Be seeing you, Callie."

After he'd stepped back and closed the door, Callie looked out her rearview mirror and noticed the motorcycle sitting behind her car.

The sight of the familiar bike drew her out of the car before she had time to consider the wisdom of her actions.

"You still have your Indian?" She slowed her steps as she neared the motorcycle, taking in every ounce of well-known detail. "It still looks like it just came out of the factory. How old is it now?"

"Over forty."

"You've taken good care of it." She ran her finger along the Indian head logo on the gas tank.

"Before my father passed this motorcycle on to me, he made me promise to take good care of it." He swung one leg up and over the bike. Sitting down, he was now at eye level with her. "When I make a commitment, Ms. Harrison, I keep it."

Callie shuddered at the contempt and accusations she saw in his eyes. But she didn't blame him. She was the one who had broken the commitment between them.

She fought back tears as she watched him fit a full-face helmet over his head and pull down the visor, blocking her out.

Turning away, she walked to her car. Back in the driver's seat, Callie started the engine. She made a U-turn and headed toward town. In her rearview mirror, she watched Rorke start his bike and follow after her.

She loved to watch him ride. It was hard to tell where the man ended and the bike began, like a twentieth-century mechanical centaur. There was a freedom about them—the freedom of a man moving faster than his two legs could take him and moving without the shell of a car between him and the elements.

Callie hadn't been on the back of any motorcycle except Rorke's, and that had been a long time ago. But the memories were still vivid. Sometimes she had just watched panoramic views sail by, the wind beating against her. Or sometimes she had just laid her head against Rorke's back and looked down, watching the yellow center line markings unroll mile after mile.

It had been wonderful. She momentarily longed for a taste of that remembered freedom, but it didn't take her long to realize—God help her—what she was longing for was to be close to Rorke.

When they got to O'Neil Automotive, Callie noticed a rental car parked out front. Continuing to watch in her rearview mirror, she saw Rorke smoothly turn into the driveway. As he pulled in, the driver of the car jumped out and went running up to him. The man was wearing a business suit and had a briefcase in tow.

Callie wondered what was going on. Obviously the man had been waiting for Rorke. She hoped he wasn't in any trouble. She thought about turning around and going back. *Don't be foolish. Whatever it is, isn't any of your business.* She continued on toward Rachel's house.

Her quest hadn't been a complete loss after all. Although nothing was really settled between the two of them, at least the next few weeks would be more pleasant. After that she would be going back to New York and she could bundle the pain up and bury it away, for good, with the memories that caused it.

Two weeks…she just had to get through two weeks.

Two weeks at work with a deadline always seemed to fly by, but would the next two weeks while she was here in Harrison be as cooperative?

Rachel Duque flew out her front door as soon as Callie pulled into her driveway. After exchanging greetings and unloading Callie's suitcases, the two women sat out back on the patio.

"So, how was the drive?"

"Not bad."

"Good, then you won't be too tired for this evening."

"This evening?" She hoped the evening agenda didn't include Rorke. She wasn't up to seeing him again, yet.

"The bridesmaids are coming over after dinner and we're going to roll scrolls and make rice bags."

"I think I can handle that. So how are the plans going?"

"Good." Rachel looked down. Her smile faded. "Umm..."

After long years of friendship, Callie knew Rachel was debating how to sugarcoat something unpleasant.

"Callie, about your father's invitation to the wedding..."

"Hey, I told you not to worry about it. I understand why your parents felt obligated to invite him. I'm sure the two of us can be in the same room together without causing problems."

"I know, but actually...you see..." Rachel was looking everywhere but at her.

"Rach, will my father be at the wedding?"

Rachel sighed and shook her head. "No. He sent a gift with a note that said his work schedule prevents him from accepting the invitation. I'm sorry, Callie."

Callie shrugged. Her father did have a busy schedule and he usually worked Saturday afternoons, but since he was the boss, he could have changed his plans if he'd wanted to. She felt safe in assuming his refusal to do so had something to do with her, unless it was because Rorke was also going to be in the wedding.

"Don't be sorry. None of it is your fault. At least he sent a gift," she joked.

"Not sending one would have been a breach of etiquette. Can you imagine Chandler Harrison not obeying etiquette?"

"He'd be more likely to defy the laws of gravity than risk having Miss Manners take him to task."

Callie could laugh about the rigid structure of the Harrison household now, but it had been a trial when she'd been growing up. Grandmother Harrison had been the one who'd taught her and her Harrison cousins. Grandmother made sure they all remembered they were Harrisons. Direct descendants of the town's founder—no matter that many other townsfolk had Harrison blood passed on through the female line—they had the name.

With the name came certain rules and responsibilities, shoulds and should nots, royal edicts covering every aspect of daily life. Of course, since her father had disowned her, technically she probably wasn't expected to maintain Harrison protocol.

"Who *is* coming to the wedding?"

"Almost everyone else who was invited." Rachel listed some familiar names and caught Callie up on some of the current goings-on around town.

"I saw the Yankee Motorworks plant."

"What were you doing on Jackson Road?"

"Taking the scenic route," Callie improvised, so she wouldn't have to admit she'd gone to see Rorke.

"Did you see the house, too?"

"House?"

"It's on Jackson between the plant and town. Almost directly across from Harrison Manor."

"I was watching the road." Her mind had been focused on Rorke. She hadn't noticed anything other than what she'd needed to drive safely.

"It's huge. I don't see how you could have missed it. Of course it is on a hill, and if you didn't happen to look up..." Rachel continued. "You can see part of it from the guest room upstairs." She stood and led the way.

Callie followed.

Looking out the guest room window, Callie recognized the land immediately—Duncan's Woods. But where there should have been solid trees there was now a house. From the bare graded ground surrounding it and the assortment of trucks in the large driveway, she guessed it was still under construction.

"The Duncans are building a new house? From the size of it they must have won a lottery."

Rachel laughed. "No, they didn't win a lottery. They sold the property to Yankee Motorworks. That's who's building the house," Rachel explained.

"The Duncans sold part of their farm?" Callie was stunned. There had been Duncans farming in the area almost as long as there had been Harrisons in Harrison, Vermont.

"They sold almost all of it except the few acres around their house."

"Sold all of it to a motorcycle millionaire?" Duncan's Woods had been a favorite meeting spot for her and Rorke. Especially the meadow tucked away within. From the angle she was at, and with the house blocking the view, she couldn't tell if the meadow was still there or not.

"You should see this guy. He's gorgeous. He was here for the ground breaking at the plant, but hasn't been back since."

"Maybe he's waiting for the house to be finished."

"It's almost done."

"How do you know?"

"Steve's the one he contracted to build it."

"Steve's building it? Have you been inside?"

"Yes, it's gorgeous. I'll check with him. Maybe he'll give us a tour."

The tour had sounded like a good idea, but the next afternoon when they arrived, Callie had second thoughts. Parked in the shade of a tree was Rorke's Indian.

Unaware of Callie's turmoil, Rachel said, "Rorke is here. I hope that means he and Steve have been in for their final tuxedo fitting."

They got out of the car and headed toward the house. Steve met them at the front door.

"Callie. Good to see you." Steve gave her a friendly hug before turning to give Rachel a quick kiss hello.

"What do you think? Didn't I tell you it was gorgeous?" Rachel asked Callie.

Callie looked around the spacious entryway. Work was still in progress, but it was easy to picture the finished beauty. The interior had an open, airy elegance that was inviting, despite its vastness. "It's lovely."

"Wait until you see the rest," Rachel said.

"This way." Steve gestured to a doorway. From the entryway, they went into the living room.

The first thing Callie noticed was Rorke.

"You remember Callie Harrison, don't you?" Steve asked Rorke.

Rorke acknowledged her with a curt nod. "Actually, I don't think we've ever been introduced."

This was his idea of a truce? Although he hadn't lied—they had never been formally introduced—it seemed like a lie of omission. She was glad Rorke wasn't one to kiss and tell, but he could have acknowledged they'd known each other, without giving anything away to the other couple.

"Never been introduced? I can fix that." Steve performed the introductions with a flourish. "Callie, may I present Rorke O'Neil. Rorke, Ms. Calista Meredith Harrison . . . one of *the* Harrisons of Harrison, Vermont."

"What a ham." Rachel rolled her eyes.

"Nice to meet you," Rorke said politely.

"My pleasure," Callie answered automatically, addressing his shoulder.

"There's a topic with potential," Rorke returned.

Her breath caught in her throat. Was he flirting with her? Her widening gaze immediately locked with his.

No, he wasn't flirting. His eyes held only cool indifference.

"Now, Rorke...stop teasing," Rachel scolded.

Rorke turned to look at Rachel. Callie was grateful to be free of his unsettling scrutiny.

The smile he gave Rachel was warm, friendly—so different from the way he'd looked at her. "What makes you think I was teasing?"

"You'd better be teasing! I don't want you scaring Callie away before the wedding," Rachel said with mock severity.

Steve laughed. "Callie's a big-city girl now. I think it would take more than that to scare her away."

Looking away from Rorke, Callie glanced around the room. Across the front wall were two large picture windows offering an awe-inspiring view. To the right, the town of Harrison lay below, nestled into its valley surrounded by rolling hillsides.

The trees were all green now, but Callie knew that in autumn they would provide a spectacular display of dappled leaves, as if a mass of squirt-gun-wielding children had been busy with red and yellow paint, which, when mixed together, made for every imaginable shade of red, orange and yellow. And in winter their bare branches would sparkle and glisten with ice.

Rising above the treetops, the tall white steeple of St. Paul's Church marked the center of town. Rachel and Steve were getting married there. Callie tried to visualize herself walking calmly up the aisle in front of Rachel while Steve stood at the altar with his best man by his side.

Best man. Yes, Rorke had her vote for *best man.* Not man in the sense of the Madison Avenue businessmen she worked around and came in contact with on a daily basis, but *man* as in male of his species.

"Guess there's more than one castle in the kingdom now." Rorke broke into her thoughts.

Straight across the valley on the opposite hill, stood Harrison Manor—a brick-and-stone sentinel keeping watch from its great height. The house where Callie had grown up. The house where, as far as she knew, her father still lived.

"Harrison Manor isn't a castle." She tried to sound normal; she didn't want to give him the satisfaction of knowing he was unnerving her.

"Of course it's a castle . . . complete with a beautiful golden-haired, blue-eyed princess." It could have been a compliment, but the look of disdain on Rorke's face made it clear it wasn't meant to be one.

From Rachel and Steve's laughter, Callie assumed that they thought Rorke was joking. But she knew better, and she was not amused. "Let's see the rest of the motorcycle millionaire's castle," she said to Steve.

They finished touring the ground floor. Steve's pride of workmanship was apparent as he pointed out various features and detailing. Next he led them upstairs. The second floor was as impressive as the first. One or more of the spare bedrooms would undoubtedly be for guests, but Callie felt sure there were children somewhere in the future of this house.

There was nothing specific to prove it, just a feeling this was a good place to raise a family. A meadow out back for playing football, trees to climb, the brook to wade in, willow branches to hide behind.

Oh, God—the willow tree.

"I've saved the best for last." Steve's voice cut into her tortured thoughts. Callie was grateful for something else to occupy her mind. She walked through the open double doors at the end of the hallway.

In keeping with the rest of the house, the master bedroom suite was huge. Callie glanced appreciatively at the marble fireplace, but found herself being drawn, against her will, to the windows on the backside of the house.

In every other room at the rear of the house, she'd managed to ignore the windows. But here in the master suite, French doors leading out to a small balcony refused to be ignored. Callie opened them and slipped outside.

She wondered if the soon-to-be-occupants would take their morning coffee here, or whether they would go out to watch the sunset in the evening. What would they be thinking as they looked out over Rorke and Callie's meadow?

Callie looked down and easily found what she was looking for. It was still there, right where she'd known it would be—the large weeping willow standing alone next to a small meandering brook.

The place where Rorke had kissed her for the first time. A kiss so different from the awkward kisses she'd experienced until then. A kiss that had awakened powerful yearnings.

Callie shuddered as she remembered the innocent wonder she'd felt back then. It had been the first kiss of many. Ironically, on another night, their last kiss had taken place beneath the same tree.

"Look at this skylight." Rachel's voice carried from inside the bedroom to where Callie stood. "I'll bet the bed is going against this wall."

"Making love in the moonlight. Not a bad idea," Steve teased.

"Of course for variety, they could go down to the brook. It looks like a nice place to make love."

Callie gasped. While her thoughts had wandered through the past, Rorke had joined her on the balcony. He leaned casually against the railing, as he, too, looked down at the meadow.

"I think I may even have made love there myself...once." He kept his voice low, so only she could hear him. Low, but sexy, sending shivers down her spine. Across the years she heard his voice teasing, laughing, confiding, sharing, husky with need and exploding with passion.

She knew he'd made love by the brook—she'd been there, underneath the weeping willow, streaks of moonlight filtering through the breeze-tossed branches, the soothing burble of water rolling over rocks providing nature's background music to whispered words of love.

Closing her eyes against the scene below them and the memories it stirred, she caught her bottom lip between her teeth and wished to be anywhere but here, with anyone but the man standing beside her.

"Why did you follow me out here? What do you want from me?" Despite her resolve to look unruffled, her voice quivered.

He shrugged. "I came out for the same reason you did—to look at the view. What do I want from you?" He laughed harshly. "Not a damn thing, sweetheart, not a damn thing." Without a glance in her direction, he strode back into the house.

Callie watched him walk away. He still carried himself with the blend of defiant confidence that had set him apart from the rest of the town. Every step, every movement of his body, was achingly familiar.

She took a deep cleansing breath and tried to stop the pain, but she was getting no breaks as long-suppressed memories rolled through her mind like a VCR gone crazy.

"Callie, you've got to see this bathroom." Rachel called to her.

Pulling back her shoulders, Callie pushed her mental turmoil to the back of her mind. The tour would be over soon; then she and Rachel would be leaving and she could think this mess through without Rorke's disturbing presence.

Reentering the house, she followed the sound of Rachel's voice into the master bath. Two steps led up to a sunken tub the size of a small swimming pool. A separate shower stall was at the far end of the room. A long double sink and vanity took up another wall.

"My whole bathroom would fit in this linen closet!" Rachel said. "And check out this tub." Rachel grabbed Callie's arm and pulled her up the steps.

"Certainly plenty of room to stretch out comfortably." Callie looked up at the ceiling above. "What, no skylight?" she quipped, trying to sound more lighthearted than she felt.

Rachel laughed. Callie turned to start back down the steps, but stopped when she saw Rorke standing in the doorway. He quickly wiped his face free of any emotions, but not before Callie had seen a hungry spark of desire.

She was surprised the sight of the meadow could have an effect on him. There had probably been any number of women during the past ten years—not to mention the women who'd been before her. Women with much more experience than she'd had. For all she knew he might be involved with someone, engaged or even married. He wasn't wearing a ring, but that wasn't always proof positive. Oblivious to the silent exchange taking place, Rachel spoke up. "This is quite a setup. Have you found out yet if he's married?"

Steve picked up Rachel's left hand and held it in front of her. "You don't have to worry about it, honey. You're taken."

"I know, but I have single friends. Callie for instance."

Rorke laughed. "You want to set Callie up with—" what was it she called him "—the motorcycle millionaire? From princess in one castle to queen in the other."

"Rorke, what did I tell you about teasing Callie?" Rachel scolded playfully. "So, is he married Steve?" she persisted.

He shrugged. "Truthfully, I have no idea."

"Does he wear a wedding ring?"

"I didn't get close enough to look."

"Even when you were going over the blueprints?"

"I deal strictly with his architect and his interior designer."

"He doesn't come to check on progress?" Callie asked.

"If he does, it's after hours or on weekends." The sound of voices traveled up from downstairs. "The guys must be back from lunch. Time to get to work."

Steve escorted them back to the entryway. While Rachel and Steve lingered inside to say their goodbyes privately, Callie and Rorke went out.

Callie watched as Rorke walked to Steve's truck and reached into the front seat. He pulled out a motorcycle helmet. The same one she'd seen him with yesterday.

"You wear a helmet now?" she asked, before considering the advisability of starting up a conversation.

"Some of us get wiser as we get older," Rorke threw back at her as he walked over to his bike.

She placed her hands on her hips. "Obviously, your definition of a truce and mine are two different things."

Three

Rorke stopped and turned to face her, taking a similar hands-on-hips stance. "I think it would be safe to say we'd put different meanings on more words than *truce,* Ms. Harrison."

"I thought we'd agreed that our private conflicts wouldn't interfere with the wedding."

"We did, and they haven't."

"All that talk about castles, princesses and...and my pleasure?" She felt the warmth of blood rushing to her cheeks. "Rachel's going to catch on, if you keep it up."

"You heard her. She thinks I was teasing."

"I know you weren't."

He lifted one dark brow and gave her a cool smile. "That's your problem, then, isn't it?" The sound of

Rachel coming out the front door, kept her from saying more. She turned and headed for the car.

"Were you two arguing?" Rachel asked as she and Callie started down the driveway.

"What would we have to argue about?" Callie laughed, hoping it didn't sound forced.

"That's what I wanted to know."

"Well, we weren't arguing."

They turned onto the road into town, riding in silence until Rachel said, "Remember what a hell-raiser Rorke was in high school?"

"I remember."

"You have to admit, he looked damn sexy in that black leather jacket. I'll bet he still does."

"Rachel!"

"Oh, come on, Callie, didn't you think he was 'totally awesome,' to quote my sixth-grade students? When he arrived at the school bus stop to offer some girl a ride, don't tell me you never wished it could be you?"

Callie shrugged. Rorke had graduated a couple of years before Callie, Rachel and Steve. He would occasionally arrive when the final bell for the day rang, to pick up whichever lucky coed had his attention that week. Blonde, brunette, redhead—he didn't seem to have a preference, but none of them kept his interest long. There were also plenty of rumors about him and girls from nearby towns. And then there were the rumors about the two of them....

"Go ahead and admit it, Callie. I don't think there was a female student at Harrison High who didn't wonder what it would be like to ride with Rorke."

Like all the rest, Callie had wondered. But unlike most of the other *nice* girls, she'd gotten to find out.

"At first it feels like you've been picked up by a whirlwind, and then you find your arms are wrapped around a powerful eagle with the strength to fly you up to heaven and then back to earth."

A feeling similar to the experience of making love with him.

Callie hadn't realized she'd spoken out loud until Rachel's gasp of surprise brought her back to the present.

"Calista Harrison, you *did* ride with Rorke!"

"Yes," Callie admitted.

"How could you and not tell me?"

Callie bit her tongue. *Darn, how was she going to talk her way out of this one?*

She settled on explaining about the first time she'd ridden with Rorke. How a flat tire and a stubborn lug nut had sent her to the O'Neil garage for help, and rather than using the gas in the tow truck she and Rorke had ridden back to her car on his motorcycle.

"And that's what set off all those rumors," Rachel said, speculating.

"I guess someone must have seen us." Callie knew no one had seen them that night. In fact, there had been many times they hadn't been seen.

"Well, why didn't you just explain what happened instead of denying it?"

Callie hadn't wanted anyone intruding on what she and Rorke had, not even her best friend. "It seemed easier to say it never happened."

"You might be right. Your father would have had a conniption. But you could at least have told me. Some best friend," she teased.

"Speaking of friends . . . when did Rorke and Steve become friends?"

"The summer after we graduated from high school, the two of them ended up enlisting in the air force together."

"The air force?" It was hard to picture the free-spirited, nonconforming Rorke submitting to anything as regimented as the military.

They arrived in downtown Harrison and parked in front of the bridal shop. Over the course of the afternoon, as she and Rachel went about winding up preparations for the big day, Callie renewed old acquaintances. Everyone from the florist to the produce man at the grocery store welcomed her home.

She even went into Harrison Bank so Rachel could deposit checks received as wedding gifts. Callie spoke briefly to several cousins and her uncle, but didn't make the long walk down the darkly paneled hallway to her father's office.

She had been thinking about visiting him on this trip, possibly trying to mend the rift between them. Not so he would put her back in his will—she didn't care if he did that or not—but he was her flesh and blood, and they had been close once.

But seeing Rorke had opened old wounds and made her unsure whether she was ready to forgive her father. She didn't even know if she could ever forgive him. . . .

* * *

Several days passed with no sign of Rorke; any time they were away from Rachel's house, Callie kept an uneasy lookout for him.

Out of sight was not out of mind in this case. She found herself unable to stop thinking about him... wondering where he was, what he was doing. She'd heard people say your first love always had a special place in your heart. Dismally she admitted they were right.

Her next encounter with Rorke came on Thursday evening when he arrived to help Steve move some of the boxes Rachel had packed up. After the wedding, the couple would be living in what was now Steve's house. Rachel was leaving most of her furniture to be sold with the house she'd shared with her first husband, but was taking her personal items and a few antiques her grandmother had given her.

Rorke's greeting was casual, aimed at both women. No sign of hostility or other strong emotion in his eyes as they met Callie's across the room. At least that was a relief.

It had been decided that after the moving chores, the four of them would have a barbecue at Steve's. With the men manning the grill and the women fixing side dishes in the kitchen, dinner was ready in no time.

They ate on a picnic table in the backyard. With Rachel and Steve cozy on one side, Callie took her place next to Rorke. While there was a respectable distance between them, he was close enough for her to feel the heat of him. Heat her own body absorbed and magnified, until she felt feverish.

She tried to act nonchalant, but every move he made drew her attention. She realized the two of them had never sat down together for a meal. She had no idea what his favorite foods were, whether he was a picky eater or one of those men who would eat anything set before him.

Even ten years ago she had known little about the details of his daily life. If they'd gotten married, she would know all these details and many others: whether he squeezed the toothpaste tube in the middle, whether he put his clothes in the hamper or dropped them wherever they happened to come off, which side of the bed he slept on....

The conversation at the table was casual and light-hearted. To an observer, Callie was sure the evening would look like a normal get-together of four old friends. But the inner strength she was calling upon to hold up her end of the facade was draining her energy. She wondered if it was as hard on Rorke. He was showing no signs of stress.

As Steve was helping himself to more fries, he said, "Callie, if you ever decide to give up commercial art, you can go into business as a psychic."

Callie wasn't sure she'd heard him right. "What?"

"I had a call today from the motorcycle millionaire's architect. He's decided he wants a skylight over the tub in the master bathroom."

"You're kidding," Rachel said. "That was Callie's idea." Rachel looked to her friend. "Maybe you are psychic."

"Or maybe the place is bugged," Callie said.

Steve whistled, a long slow whistle. "I hadn't thought about that." He frowned.

"Now don't get worried, Steve. It was a joke," Callie said.

"I'm sure it was just an interesting coincidence," Rorke said. "Why would anyone bug a construction site?"

"Maybe you should stick around and meet this guy, Callie," Rachel suggested. "He may be your soul mate."

Callie and Steve laughed. Rorke was quiet and seemed to be singularly interested in the food on his plate.

Rachel continued. "Just think, if you married him, you could move back to Harrison and it could be just like old times."

Callie looked at Rachel. "There are times when I really miss Harrison. Especially when I'm running late and can't find a cab."

"Give up the rat race, then. Come back home," Rachel urged. "Rorke, you've just moved back. Tell Callie how wonderful it is to be home."

Rorke had just moved back?

Where had he been? How long had he been gone? Maybe this was why he didn't know she and her father were no longer on speaking terms. Callie glanced at Rorke. He was watching her, but his emotions were carefully masked. He was definitely not open to questions, and she couldn't tell how he felt about Rachel's suggestion that she move back to Harrison... whether he liked the idea, hated the idea or was totally indifferent.

"Callie's a big girl, Rachel. I'm sure she's capable of making her own decisions. Even if she's not, I don't think she'd appreciate someone else making them for her."

Callie caught Rorke's subtle criticism, but she bit her tongue and ignored it. *If she made it through the next week without losing her temper, surely she would be nominated for some type of award.* "Besides, if I moved back, what excuse would you use to go shopping in New York?"

"I'd just say I needed to do some shopping, and I'd probably drag you along with me. Didn't you say someone you work with just had a baby and is working out of her apartment now? Why can't you do the same thing?"

Rachel made it sound so easy. And doing her job long-distance probably was the easy part when compared to the fortitude it would take to live where she would be running into Rorke.

"It's probably feasible, but—"

Steve took Rachel's hand in his. "Rachel, like Rorke said, Callie's a big girl and can make up her own mind."

Rachel shrugged. "I know, but it's so good to have you here, Callie. Back in our old stomping grounds. There are so many memories here."

It was ironic that Rachel didn't know the true extent of her words.

Memories, yes, there were many memories here in Harrison. Good memories, not-so-good memories and, of course, memories of Rorke. The memories Callie had locked up tightly the night she'd driven away. Memories that were slowly rising to haunt her.

"I'll think about it, Rachel." Callie's answer was noncommittal.

"Great. Anyone ready for dessert?"

Steve groaned. Callie and Rorke also declined. They all pitched in to clear the table and stow the leftovers in the refrigerator.

With everything back in order, they went into the living room. Rachel and Steve sat on the couch side by side. Callie sat on the love seat and Rorke chose a chair.

"Is anything on TV tonight?" Rachel picked up the magazine of television listings and started thumbing through it. "Wow, come look at this, Callie."

Callie went over to the couch, sat down next to Rachel and took the magazine she offered. It was opened to an advertisement for Yankee Motorworks. "I saw the billboard the other morning . . . very pleasant layout." The ad was much smaller than the billboard, but its physical effect on her was just as startling.

"Pleasant layout? Give me a break!" Steve laughed. "Don't tell me it's professional artist's interest. You're looking at the guys, don't try to deny it."

"The guys *are* nice, but . . ."

"Nice?" Rachel cut in, taking the magazine out of Callie's hands. "Nice? This is the stuff of dreams." She punctuated her words by tapping her index finger on the glossy photo.

Steve placed one hand melodramatically over his heart. "You wound me deeply, my dear." He took the magazine from Rachel and tossed it across the room to Rorke. "What do you think, pal?"

After making an effortless catch, Rorke looked down at the picture. "Is this the stuff of your dreams, too, Callie?" He couldn't know, could he? Of course not. Nobody could know she'd had several dreams of the man in white.

Dreams of him swooping down and scooping her up on his motorcycle, holding her in front of him. He never spoke, but she could feel him watching her from inside his helmet. When she reached up to push back the darkened visor, the dream would dissolve around her and she would find herself awake. Awake, but with a gnawing sense of loss.

She hadn't answered Rorke's question. Rachel and Steve were also looking at her, waiting for an answer. "I think most women would find the ad visually appealing. What's not to like?"

"That's not what I asked," Rorke replied. His eyes sent her a private challenge.

Was he trying to find out if images of motorcycles affected her? If they set off memories of what they'd been through together in the past? Of what she would still have if she'd stayed with him? Since he claimed to be indifferent to her, she didn't understand his need to know her reaction to the picture, but he seemed determined to get her answer.

"Dream material? All right, I'll admit it, there's dream material in that photo," she told him honestly. "But I've met enough male models in my years in New York to know that beauty, as they say, is only skin deep."

Hmm, maybe she should make a few phone calls and find out who the models in the picture were. Perhaps the mystique of the white knight would be shattered.

Then she'd have only one leather-clad motorcycle rider on her troubled mind, and she'd had plenty of practice pushing thoughts of him into the background.

Steve pulled up his arm to show off his biceps. "They probably got their builds working out in a gym somewhere instead of carrying two-by-fours and swinging a hammer like a real man."

Rachel looked suitably impressed.

They talked a while longer. When Callie started yawning, Rachel suggested they leave.

Steve pointed to the boxes stacked against the wall. "I thought you were going to do something with those?"

"Callie's tired. I'll come back tomorrow," Rachel said.

"I'm sure I can stay awake long enough to help you unpack," Callie said.

Rachel started to stand. "There's really no hurry."

"Listen, if you'd like to stay, I can drop Callie off on my way home," Rorke offered.

Callie wanted to refuse for her own sake, but she could tell from the look that passed between them that Rachel and Steve were grateful for the chance to be alone. With Callie staying at Rachel's and all the preparations for the wedding, they'd had little time for just the two of them.

Callie wondered if Steve and Rorke had prearranged his offer. Regardless, she felt obligated to accept. She smiled politely. "I'd appreciate it. Thanks, Rorke."

"No problem."

They said their goodbyes, and Callie and Rorke headed out the door. As Steve closed it quietly behind them, Callie felt a twinge of envy. Tonight Steve and

Rachel were grabbing a few hours alone, but soon they would be married, living under the same roof, and they would go through each day knowing that in the evening there would be someone there for them. Someone who cared...

"I noticed your car at Rachel's. Is that where you'd like me to take you?" Rorke's voice broke into her thoughts.

Take me to heaven and back.

"Rachel's is fine. That's where I'm staying."

They walked, several feet apart to Rorke's motor-cycle.

"I didn't know I'd have a rider tonight, so I've only got one helmet with me. It might be too big, but it will have to do."

Before she could protest, he had the helmet over her head and was adjusting the chin strap. His fingers were warm as they brushed against her neck, sending sparks skittering through her.

When he was done, he got on the bike and held out his hand to her as he'd done so many times in the past.

She looked down at the motorcycle seat and couldn't avoid looking at the seat of Rorke's blue jeans as well. Unbidden, she remembered a survey she'd read that had listed good buns as one of the physical attributes women noticed first on a man. Rorke would certainly score top marks in that department. Not to mention well-muscled thighs, broad shoulders, killer blue eyes...

"Sweetheart, we don't have all night."

Callie's gaze flew to meet his. She was embarrassed at being caught studying his anatomy. Especially when she could see him fighting back a smile.

After a deep breath for courage, she put her hand in his. It felt warm and familiar in shape, but it was smoother, less callused, than she remembered. He pulled her gently forward. Callie put one foot on the rear footpeg, swung the other leg up and climbed on behind him, sitting well back on the seat.

"Will you slide forward?" She could hear the laughter in his voice.

She moved up a few more inches, but it still wasn't enough to satisfy him. He reached his arms back. Spreading one large palm on each side of her behind, he pulled her forward until she was tight against him.

Closing her eyes, she let the old sensations wash over her. From shoulders to knees, she was pressed intimately against him. The hard warmth of his hands, lingering longer than necessary on her derriere, added to her discomfort as long-dormant nerve endings sparked into action. She reached her arms around his waist and clasped her hands over his firm stomach.

"Ready?" His voice was muffled by the helmet over her ears, but she thought it sounded gruffer than usual.

"Ready."

He started the engine and they were off.

She couldn't lay her head against his back with the helmet on, so the temptation to do so was easily resisted. It was much harder to keep her hands in one place, denying them the pleasure of roaming over solid, male muscle.

It was several miles between Steve's and Rachel's, but it seemed they were there in no time. Rorke helped her off the bike and removed the helmet, setting it on the seat. He walked to the door with her.

Callie ached to be taken into his arms and kissed. Kissed in the way only Rorke could kiss her. Until her body cried out for relief and her mind stopped analyzing. Until she was completely out of control.

It had come close to overwhelming her at eighteen but she was older now and longed for the surrender of power, knowing it would give a momentary escape from the guilt and pain of the past. *But she couldn't invite him in to seduce her, or vice versa.*

"Would you like to come in for coffee?"

Four

——

"**I**'d better not."

"Oh?" Was he feeling as drawn to her as she was to him? Was he afraid if he came in he would end up giving in to his desire?

He tucked his hands into the pockets of his jeans. "Yes, we've got several early appointments coming into the garage in the morning."

Disappointment settled over her. How could she have thought he'd meant anything else? "Well, I won't keep you, then. Thanks for the ride." She unlocked the door and stepped inside. Turning she said, "Good night, Rorke."

For several moments he stood quietly looking down at her.

Other parting scenes between them passed through

Callie's mind. After his "Good night, Callie," Rorke would add, "Dream of me."

Callie always answered, "I will." And most nights she *had* dreamed of him.

But tonight all Rorke said was "Good night, Callie." Then he turned and walked away from her.

A sense of panic seized her and she had to fight to keep from calling out to him. She felt her bottom lip begin to quiver and tears fill her eyes.

She quickly closed the door between them...before he could turn and see how his leaving was affecting her.

Leaning back against the closed door with her fists clenched and her arms crossed over her stomach, she tried to separate the emotions flooding her.

The physical arousal that riding with Rorke had caused was hard to ignore but easy to understand. After all, he'd been the first to awaken her to the physical side of love.

But she didn't understand the panic she'd felt when he'd turned to go. She felt fear...but of what? And then the need to cry...why? Because he hadn't agreed to come in? Because he was leaving? Because he seemed immune to her physically when she ached for him? Because she knew in one more week she would be leaving, and she might never see him again? Or was it simply regret for what she'd been forced to give up?

As upset as she was, once Callie was upstairs in bed, she managed to fall asleep. She slept peacefully until the early hours of the morning when the sound of a motorcycle engine grew louder, and the biker in white leather rode through the mist into her dream.

This time she tried to run, but she didn't get far and once again found herself in his arms.

Instead of continuing down the road with her, he stopped and shifted her around to face him, sitting her so she straddled the gas tank, her knees hooked over his muscular thighs.

She could feel heat, burning her through the layers of his leather and her silky nightgown.

Placing her open hands on the front of his jacket, she felt warmth there also. She looked down at her hands against the soft, white leather. As she watched, the area around her fingers turned black. Moving in slow waves the color spread outward until the whole jacket was black.

She saw his pants and helmet had also turned black. Every breath was a struggle. Slowly she tried to shake her head no. She could see her reflection in his visor.

It was time to see what was behind it. Callie reached her hands up. He didn't try to stop her, but he didn't offer any assistance, either.

She unclasped the latch under his chin, aware of the heat of his skin and the rasp of whisker stubble. Pressing her fingers against the pulse in his neck, she felt the strong beating of his heart. Taking a steadying breath, she began pushing the helmet up.

When it was all the way off, holding it in one hand, she lowered it to her side, then released it. It made a soft thud as it hit the ground.

She looked up.

He had the face to match the gorgeous body. By her standards, it was the most handsome face she'd ever seen.

She sat up in bed—her heart pounding, her breathing rapid and shallow.

She dropped her head into her hands and ran her fingers through her hair.

Turning to the side, she looked at the clock. It was too early to call anyone and begin the search for the Yankee ad model's identity, but she promised herself she would find out who the man in white was before she slept again.

On Friday morning, she hung up the kitchen phone, shaking her head. Callie's hope for ending the dreams by learning the identity of the model was short-lived.

Rachel shuffled into the room, yawning. "Good morning." She blinked and tried to open her eyes wider. "Are you okay? I know I'm half asleep, but you look a bit pale."

"You're not going to believe what I just found out." Callie walked over and sat down at the kitchen table.

Rachel sat across from her. "What?"

"Remember the Yankee Motorworks ad we were looking at last night at Steve's?"

Rachel made a purring sound. "Of course I remember."

"Well . . . the guys in the picture are not egotistical male models." There went her chance for peace and relief.

"They're not? Then who are they?"

"You can't tell anyone."

"You're kidding?"

"No. The picture is taking the country by storm and speculation is flying about who the men are."

"So how did you find out?"

"I made a few calls to locate the firm that handles the Yankee account, then called a friend who works there, pandered to his ego a bit, and he told me. He's gloating over the ad's success, I got the feeling he was dying to show someone how clever he's been."

"Are you going to keep me in suspense all day?"

"The men in the photo are the three company founders."

Rachel was awake now. "Three motorcycle millionaires?"

"Yep, three of them. All blessed with animal magnetism and worth a fortune to boot."

"Wow."

"Of course we haven't seen their faces—that might be why they chose to be photographed with full-face helmets," Callie said.

"The one who was here for the ground breaking was a hunk. We could go to the *Harrison Outlook* office and get a copy of the article covering the ground breaking so you could see him. Plus, I'll bet we could find pictures of all three in back issues of magazines or larger newspapers."

Callie admitted the idea was tempting. "Rachel, the last time we looked up pictures of guys we were in high school. Haven't we outgrown that kind of thing?"

"But that was when we were looking up movie stars we didn't have a chance of ever meeting. One of these motorcycle guys is going to be living right here in Harrison, in a gorgeous house with your skylight over the tub."

"All the more reason we shouldn't go drooling over his picture like a couple of teenagers." And in the clear light of day a small part of her wasn't sure she was

ready to give up the fantasy. As long as she didn't
know what he really looked like, he could be as out-
rageously attractive as she could imagine him.

"If you expect to be drooling, you must think
they're all gorgeous?"

"With that body it would be a bad joke if he
wasn't."

"*He?* You have a favorite? Which one?"

Callie shrugged. What could it hurt to tell Rachel
the truth? "The one in white."

"I wonder if he's the one who's coming to Harrison?"

She couldn't help picturing the man in white in the
house—even though it was only a one-in-three chance
the house was going to be his. She could see him
stretched out in the large tub, underneath the skylight
she'd thought of...standing on the balcony, looking
out over the meadow...and maybe one night he would
take a women down to the brook and make love to her
under the weeping willow tree. "I have no idea."

"We'll know when he gets here. And speaking of
motorcycles, how was your ride last night with Rorke?
As good as it was the first time?"

Callie shrugged. "It was all right." She half expected a bolt of lightning to crash through the ceiling
and strike her for such a blatant lie.

Later that afternoon, Callie drove into Exeter to buy
mauve ribbon. She and Rachel were halfway through
the process of putting small ribbon roses on the rice
bags when they'd run out of ribbon.

Neither the bridal shop nor the flower shop in Harrison had the right color. Rachel had an appointment

with the man who would be videotaping the ceremony, so Callie had offered to get the ribbon.

Returning to her car, purchase in hand, Callie noticed a familiar motorcycle parked a half block away. Without thinking of the consequences, she started walking down the street.

In the area where the bike was parked, there was a shoe repair, a dental office, a real estate office, a legal office and an accountant's office. Of course he could be anywhere on the block or even across the street.

Checking both ways for cars, Callie walked across the street and entered a bookstore. She positioned herself by the front window, where she could keep an eye on Rorke's bike while she browsed.

About five minutes later, she looked up and saw Rorke standing on the sidewalk next to his bike. Drat, she'd missed seeing where he'd been. Not that she should care . . . but she did. Standing with him was the man she'd seen the other morning at O'Neil Automotive. They appeared to be arguing.

She wondered again if Rorke was in trouble. When the stranger stormed off, Callie quickly made her way over to Rorke.

"Rorke, is everything all right?"

He looked surprised to see her, but he recovered quickly. "I don't know. I haven't had time to watch the news today."

"I didn't mean 'everything' in general, I meant everything with you?"

His eyes narrowed as he looked down at her. "I'm fine. Shouldn't I be?"

"It's just that I saw you arguing with that man." She gestured in the direction he'd gone. "I saw him the other morning at the garage...I thought you might be in some sort of trouble.''

He looked amused. ''Really?''

''Listen, if you need money—''

All signs of humor faded. ''Callie, I don't need your money.''

''A lawyer, then? I have a friend in New York. I think I have his number.'' She set the bag with the ribbon on his motorcycle seat next to his helmet, and rummaged through her purse.

''I don't need a lawyer.'' His voice was tight, the message stronger than the words he spoke.

Ignoring him, Callie continued her search. ''I know it's here somewhere.''

''Callie.'' Rorke placed his hand on her arm to stop her.

At his touch all the sensations she'd felt last night flared up again. All awareness of where they were and what she'd been doing faded away. Her gaze moved from her purse to Rorke. In the clear light of day, she could see he was feeling something, too.

They stared into each other's eyes for long, quiet moments. Slowly Rorke brought his other hand up and lay it against her cheek. She noticed again how much smoother it felt.

''Callie,'' he whispered.

She took a step toward him, starting to move her arms up to put them around his neck. Her forgotten purse slipped out of her grasp and fell between them with a thud, scattering its contents.

Rorke snapped out of his daze first, bent down, picked up her purse and began replacing the fugitive items. When he was finished he handed it back to her, without looking her in the eye. He turned, got his helmet and gave her the bag of ribbon.

Once his helmet was in place, he climbed onto the bike and started the engine.

He was leaving? Leaving without acknowledging whatever it was that had taken place between them?

"Rorke?"

"See you later," he said. He pulled away from the curb, leaving a stunned Callie staring after him.

Snapping to attention, she raced to her car and started after him. She still didn't know what kind of trouble he was in. If it were purely a matter of speed, she knew she wouldn't have a prayer. But add a few cars and several traffic lights, and she just might catch him.

Finally, at the last stoplight in town, she pulled up on his right. Raising her voice to be heard over the engines, she yelled, "Rorke, if you're in trouble, let me help you."

At first she thought he hadn't heard or was going to ignore her; then he raised up his visor. "Forget it, Callie."

"Please!"

"It's none of your business! I don't know how much clearer I can make it for you."

Whether it was clear or not, the light turned green and ended the discussion. They drove side by side until they reached the end of town and the road narrowed to one lane; then Rorke accelerated leaving Callie behind.

Who was this strange guy following him around? And why were Rorke's hands smoother? Shouldn't they be more callused after ten years of working on engines?

Too many questions . . . Callie sighed as cycle and rider disappeared in the distance.

Rorke watched Callie's car shrink away to a small dot in his rearview mirror.

He'd almost kissed her. Was he losing his mind?

He'd been proud of the resistance he'd shown last night. It had taken a lot to leave her on Rachel's doorstep with just a good-night after she'd been pressed so tightly against him. His busy schedule had kept him celibate too long, so it was perfectly understandable for his body to react to the situation. But he'd reminded his raging hormones this was not just any warm receptive female, this was Calista Harrison who'd already used him for her own benefit once and could do it again.

He promised himself a few days in New York after the wedding was over. He had several close female friends who would be more than willing to cure what ailed him, with no strings attached. He'd avoided accepting any of the offers from the women in Harrison. He was going to settle down and be a respectable citizen this time—not that he believed all the respectable citizens were as respectable behind closed doors as they let everyone else think, but he was determined to try.

This afternoon, Callie had seemed genuinely concerned for his well-being. Of course, her concern was probably fueled by guilt—assuming she had a conscience. She really had some nerve offering him money. He wondered what her reaction would be if he

told her Matt was his secretary and they'd been final-
izing contracts.

It was all straightforward, but Matt had also used
the opportunity to pressure him about Alex's bright
idea for next year's Bike Week in Daytona Beach,
Florida. It wasn't until March, but Alex wanted to get
working on advanced publicity.

Their current ad campaign had been successful.
They'd posed on a whim, never planning to reveal
their identities, but in the week since the campaign
began, things had changed.

Now Alex wanted to go public—step off the bill-
boards and out of the pages of the magazines onto
Main Street at Daytona Beach.

Alex hadn't been to Bike Week or he never would
have suggested such a thing. Yankee had been partic-
ipating in the annual event the past few years, sending a racing team and a crew with an assortment of
bikes for demo rides. But he, Alex and Jesse had never
attended.

Since the executives of their top competition put in
a good showing, Rorke had suggested they plan to do
the same. Attend and participate in some way, but not
in red, white and blue leather suits looking like comic
book super heros. The only leather he planned to wear
was black.

Jesse hadn't committed to the crazy scheme, either;
hopefully between the two of them they could make
Alex see reason.

Rorke slowed down as he entered Harrison city
limits. He cruised past Harrison Bank. Bitterness
twisted through him.

He made himself remember the women he'd been with over the past ten years, many of whom he could have again with a simple phone call. Beautiful, sophisticated women who knew how to make him feel like a king.

But they all faded away and were replaced by a vision of Callie as she'd started to reach her arms up around his neck. The golden-haired princess, who made him feel like a lowly stable boy.

Unless—his mind shifted gears—she'd wanted him to kiss her, maybe she'd like a little bedroom aerobics while she was in town. It made perfect sense for him and Callie to make love if the urge was there for both of them. He didn't know why he hadn't thought of it earlier—why he'd planned to rush off to New York for a no-strings-attached night with a friend.

The only glitch in the plan was a place. He was currently living above the garage with his father, and Callie was staying at Rachel's. He'd given up the front seat of the tow truck years ago, and while there were still plenty of secluded spots in the woods around Harrison, he wanted Callie in a bed this time.

He didn't know where or when, but he knew who and what, so a trip to Harrison Pharmacy was definitely in order.

Saturday afternoon a group of Rachel's co-workers had planned a surprise bridal shower. Callie's job had been to get Rachel there without her suspecting anything.

Callie knew many of the women—some of the younger teachers had gone to school with her and some of the older ones had been teaching when she'd been a student.

The gifts ranged from practical towels and sheets to frilly nightgowns and assorted lingerie, which stirred up a few catcalls and racy comments from the bold and set off blushes in the not-so-bold.

"Has anyone heard how the bachelor party went last night?" Rachel asked.

"Jack had a great time," one of the younger women said.

"Did he say anything about a girl in a cake?" Steve had been teasing Rachel about it for weeks.

"Yes, he did."

Rachel frowned. "I was hoping it was just a joke."

"Hey, don't worry," the woman continued. "She left the party with Rorke."

Rachel looked relieved. Callie felt a knot forming in the pit of her stomach.

"Lucky girl!" another woman said.

Rachel laughed. "June, I'm surprised at you."

"I'll tell you what. That man can hang his leather jacket on my bedpost and park his boots under my bed any day of the week."

There was a general agreement among many of the young single women in the room. Callie wasn't surprised by the women's attraction to Rorke, but she was caught off guard by the surge of jealousy shooting through her.

You had your chance and made your choice so lock up the green-eyed monster.

Of course other women were attracted to him—he was gorgeous. And it was natural they'd want to sleep with him—men don't come any sexier.

But she couldn't stop herself from hoping June never got her wish and that Rorke had given the woman from last night's bachelor party a ride home and nothing else.

"You were very quiet this afternoon," Rachel remarked as the two of them were driving back to her house.

"Not really."

"Maybe not in the beginning, but you were after Rorke's name came into the conversation."

Callie shook her head. "It's just your imagination."

"Calista Harrison, don't you try to lie to me. I know you too well. What's up?"

"Nothing."

"Did he come on to you the other night when he drove you home?"

Callie laughed. "Hardly."

"Did he stay for a while?"

"No, he walked me to the door and then left."

"Did he kiss you good-night?"

"No, he did not kiss me good-night."

Callie pulled into Rachel's driveway and stopped the car. Before she could get out, Rachel asked, "Did you want him to?"

Turning, Callie looked at her friend. She was sure the truth was written all over her face, so she admitted it. "Yes, I wanted him to kiss me."

Rachel grinned. "I knew it."

"Don't be getting any ideas."

"Who me?" Rachel opened the door and stepped out of the car.

Callie followed. "I mean it, Rachel. No match-making."

"I want you to be as happy as I am."

"I'm happy. If I was any happier, they'd lock me away in a padded room somewhere." When Rachel didn't answer, Callie continued. "Besides, I thought I was supposed to be saving myself for the motorcycle millionaire. We're soul mates, remember?"

Rachel reached the door, unlocked it and went in. She obviously had some plan brewing. Callie hoped it wasn't anything too obvious or too embarrassing. And she certainly hoped Rorke didn't think she'd put Rachel up to it.

Five

———

Callie didn't have to wait long to discover the first trick up Rachel's sleeve. The next afternoon, Rachel's car refused to start. She and Steve had an appointment with the pastor of St. Paul's. Steve could pick her up, but she needed to have the car fixed as soon as possible. Would Callie mind waiting at the house for Rorke to come and fix it?

There was no gracious way to refuse.

After Rachel and Steve left, Callie curled up on the couch with a book and tried to read—her ears tuned for the sound of Rorke's arrival. Strangely, she wasn't feeling fear or dread, but anticipation. It hit her like a runaway train that she was looking forward to seeing him again.

She set the book down and began to pace. *Don't do this to yourself, Callie. One more week and you'll be on your way home.* Emotional tangles were not on her agenda.

He'd almost kissed her Friday, or more accurately, they'd almost kissed each other. Now that the shock had worn off, she admitted how much she wished it had happened. Just to see if the old magic was still there—to see if it was as she remembered it.

In odd moments, such as now, it seemed as though the time she'd spent falling in love with Rorke had never really happened. As though it had been nothing more than a summer dream.

The sound of an engine cut into her thoughts. Looking out the window, she saw Rorke pulling up in the tow truck. She went through the kitchen, into the garage and pushed the button to open the door.

Callie savored the sight of watching him appear inch by inch, from motorcycle boots on up.

She gestured to Rachel's car. "Here's the patient," she said with forced cheerfulness.

Rorke nodded his acknowledgment. "Are the keys in the ignition?"

"No, I have them." She reached into the pocket of her jeans.

Rorke held out his hand. Callie walked over and dropped the keys into his open palm.

"Thanks." He walked to the driver's door.

"I...ah...I'll be in the house if you need anything."

He made a dismissive gesture.

Callie went back inside. Well...Friday's close call must have been caused by some strange aberration and obviously Rorke had recovered from it. There weren't any sparks or even warmth between them, only cool indifference. Without Rachel and Steve, he hadn't even bothered to be friendly.

It shouldn't hurt. She shouldn't care. But shouldn't didn't reflect the reality.

She went back into the living room and tried once again to concentrate on her book, but ended up staring into space until she heard a knock at the door that led into the garage. Popping up like a tiddlywink, she raced to answer it, then had to take a few seconds to compose herself before opening the door.

"I found the problem." Rorke's tone of voice was impersonal—an average repairman reporting to an average customer.

"That was fast."

He shrugged. "Dead battery. The headlights had been left on."

"Can you fix it?"

"I've got a new one at the garage. I'll go get it, unless that will interfere with your plans for the afternoon."

"No plans." Except perhaps considering a career change. The way she was carrying on this casual conversation, while her insides were in turmoil, convinced her she could have a promising future in Hollywood or on Broadway.

"Fine, I'll be back, then."

Callie stood in the doorway, unable to tear her gaze away from his retreating figure. Lord, he was gorgeous, but then he always had been. The way his blue jeans fit snugly across his backside. . . .

She quickly closed the door, hoping he hadn't seen her ogling him.

Knowing it was futile to even attempt going back to her book, she picked up the phone instead. Using the nonemergency number, she called the Harrison fire department. When Rachel had begun planning her wedding she had teasingly mentioned the fireworks display the night before the royal wedding of Prince Charles and Lady Di. Callie had decided to look into the idea. She'd found it relatively easy to arrange, going through the Harrison fire department since they were the ones who handled the Fourth of July and Founder's Day fireworks every year.

She spoke to one of the men on duty and reconfirmed that everything was set to go next Friday evening, including a grapevine message to let everyone but the bride and groom know about the event. They talked awhile longer, the fireman filling Callie in on some of the more current comings and goings of local residents. They were up to Miss Dunsworth's trip to Scotland when Callie heard Rorke return.

It wasn't long before he knocked. Callie ended the phone call and went to answer the door.

"The bill," Rorke said, handing Callie a slip of paper. He started to turn away.

"Just a minute. Rachel left a check."

He followed her into the kitchen. After she paid him, he said goodbye and turned to leave.

"Would you like some sun tea? Rachel made it yesterday," Callie said, surprising herself by offering. Did she really want to prolong this ordeal?

"All right." Rorke walked over to the kitchen table and sat down.

Callie was as surprised by Rorke's acceptance as she'd been by her offer. She poured tea into two ice-filled glasses. "Sugar?"

"No, straight up is fine."

After setting his glass down, she settled into the chair across from him. *Now what?* The quaint intimacy of sitting across from Rorke at a kitchen table was unsettling.

He seemed unaffected as he took a long drink of tea. Setting his glass down, he looked at her. The indifference in his eyes faded, but this time it wasn't replaced by hostility.

She couldn't read his expression, but it seemed softer. "So...how have you been?" His voice had also softened.

Callie took a deep breath and let it out slowly. She knew he wasn't asking how she'd been since Friday, but how she'd been for the past ten years. "Fine...just fine." It wasn't true, but it was a much easier answer to give than the truth. *Half alive...I've only been half alive, and I didn't even realize it until I saw you again.*

She gave him a half smile. "How about you?"

"All right."

"The other night at Steve's, Rachel said you'd recently moved back to Harrison."

"Yes, I have."

He wasn't refusing to answer her questions, but he wasn't giving her much information, either. "Where have you been living?"

"Most recently in New York City."

Her heartbeat quickened. "Really?" It was a big city, but somehow it disturbed her to think she and Rorke had been living there at the same time.

What would have happened if they'd run into each other in New York, far away from the emotionally laden atmosphere of Harrison? A small part of her rose up with the wish that he still lived in New York, but she squelched it.

Rorke nodded. "I was surprised to learn you lived there, too. Steve mentioned you're a professional artist."

"I work for an advertising firm."

"Madison Avenue? Impressive."

"It's not as glamorous as it sounds. I'm in the art department. We work out the finished product but rarely get to come up with the initial ideas."

"No matter what you're doing there, New York City and Madison Avenue are a long way from Harrison... and I'm not talking about miles."

He was right, and it was the differences between Harrison and New York that had made her choose it in the first place. Large, impersonal, a place to start over again. A place where your neighbors didn't know everything going on in your life or the lives of your family for several hundred years back. "What have you been doing there? Working on cars?"

"Motorcycles. I've been working with motorcycles."

The haunting billboard flashed into her mind. "Ever work on any Yankees?"

"Quite a few."

"What do you think of them?"

He shrugged. "They're a great bike."

"Think they can compete with the big guns?"

"Only time will tell, but so far Yankee is holding its own in the market, especially with first-time riders."

Finally, a subject he would say more than a half-dozen words about. She should have known to bring up motorcycles earlier. Rorke had always loved talking motorcycles and motorcycle history. "Have you ridden one?"

"Actually, I own one."

The vision of the biker with white leather transforming to black leather danced at the edges of her thoughts. "Really?"

One dark brow rose in question and the ice was back in his blue eyes. "Why so surprised? Don't you think I have enough money to own a new bike?"

Callie was stunned by his bitter question. She didn't remember him being touchy about money. Did he think the reason she'd left him was financial? "Th... that has nothing to do with it. It's just since I got here, all I've seen you on has been the Indian."

Rorke shrugged, releasing some of the defensive tenseness in his shoulders, and looked down at his glass. "I guess I do tend to ride it more often around town."

Callie took her first sip of tea, searching for a way to continue the conversation. "With all your motorcycle experience, have you thought about working at the Yankee plant? Especially since you own one of their bikes, I'll bet they'd be interested."

The right side of his mouth quirked up in a half smile. "They might be." He glanced at his watch.

Callie had a million other questions she longed to ask him, but since he was checking the time it seemed the enthusiasm for their conversation was one-sided. An uncomfortable silence stretched between them.

Rorke finished his tea and stood up. "Well, I'd better be going. Remind Rachel to turn off her headlights in the future."

"I will." She followed him across the kitchen, then stepped in front of him to open the door. "Oh, by the way, Rachel appreciated your assistance with the woman at the bachelor party the other night."

He smiled—a slow smile. "Well, I'm glad she appreciated it. But it didn't have anything to do with her."

Her hand froze on the doorknob. He was smiling like a bird who'd slept late, but still managed to catch the worm.

Once again Callie found herself battling jealousy as she realized how slim the chances were that he'd merely dropped the woman off at her doorstep. How could he almost kiss her Friday afternoon and then spend Friday night doing heaven knew what with someone else—and worst of all, have the nerve to look so pleased about it?

"Callie, are you all right?" Concern mingled with contained laughter in his voice.

She stepped back, leaning against the door. "I'm fine. Why shouldn't I be?"

"No reason, but you look like you've just bitten into a sour apple."

The wall between them had a crack after all. He was tuning in to her emotions and had noticed how his words had upset her. The thought sent a shiver up her spine. Had he also seen her awareness of him and her confused feelings? "Thanks again for fixing Rachel's car on short notice. I won't keep you any longer. I know you have to be getting the tow truck back to the garage." *Will you stop with the smile already?*

"It was definitely my pleasure."

Her breath caught in her throat as she remembered their exchange at the construction site. After Steve had formally introduced them, she'd said, "My pleasure." Rorke's response had stunned her, but now she found herself repeating his words. "There's a topic with potential."

Desire flared in his eyes, along with a glimpse of the Rorke she'd known so many years ago. He took a step toward her. "I was hoping you'd think so."

With arms extended, she placed her hands flat against the hard wall of his chest. She'd forgotten how lethal the full force of his charm could be. "We have a truce—remember?"

The scent of his after-shave washed over her as he stepped closer. Her elbows folded and moved back to her sides to accommodate him.

"Our truce is for angry or hostile feelings. Nothing was said about limiting anything else between us."

"Anything else?"

He reached up and covered her hands with his own, tucking his fingers around hers. "Like exploring the topic of my pleasure." He dipped down and pressed his hard lips to the wildly racing pulse at the base of her throat.

Callie leaned her head back, arching her neck toward him. "Your pleasure?" she whispered.

He looked deep into her eyes, erasing years and memories. There was no sign of love or tenderness, but plenty of male appreciation and unconcealed lust.

"And yours," Rorke said just before he moved his mouth onto hers. The touch, tentative at first, increased when he realized she wasn't going to fight him. He let go of her hands and slipped his own down to her waist, then to her back.

Tightening his arms, he pulled her close to the long, hard length of him. He opened his mouth over hers, and his tongue gently encouraged her to do the same.

It felt right, so very right, to be in his arms again. It was like stepping through a time warp, the last ten years compressing into little more than a single heartbeat. Now she felt as though she had truly come home.

She slid her hands up and around his neck, letting the ends of his dark hair curl around her fingers. With a growl that surfaced from deep in his throat, Rorke moved them until her back was pressed against the door. Leaning into her, he kept their bodies tightly aligned, while giving his hands the freedom to roam.

And roam they did...waking her nerve endings with skilled caresses.

She wasn't alone in her response to the kiss. He was as aroused as she was. The evidence pressed firmly between them.

Callie felt herself beginning to slip away. The other night, she'd thought she wanted this surrender, this escape, but as she felt her control waning, panic gripped her.

A door burst open within her. She could see something strange and beautiful beyond.... Did she want to cross the threshold...leaving the safe and familiar behind? This door had opened for her once before and she'd taken the challenge. It had been magic—almost too much magic for a naive, overprotected eighteen-year-old to handle, but how would it be now at twenty-eight?

She wondered. But it was a wonder laced with uncertainty. As though sensing her withdrawal, Rorke lifted his head, breaking the intimate contact. "Callie?"

Callie's eyes fluttered open and she looked up at him. "Rorke...I..."

The sound of a car pulling into the driveway caught her attention. "I think Steve and Rachel are back." Car doors opening and closing and voices coming closer supported her guess.

Rorke moved her away from the door and into the kitchen. He set her down in the chair she'd been sitting in earlier. *How had he known that without his support her knees would have refused to hold her?*

He was in the chair across from her, looking casual, when Steve and Rachel entered the room. How could he look so calm? Outwardly calm, but with sparks of awareness and longing smoldering in the otherwise cool blue of his eyes.

Over another round of tea, Rorke filled Rachel in on her car, and Steve suggested the four of them go to dinner and take in a movie. Callie looked at Rorke, waiting to see if he would agree. It would be the closest thing to a traditional date that they'd had with each other.

"Callie? What do you think? Shall we chaperone these two?"

Put that way, it didn't sound as much like a date—it sounded harmless enough.

"All right." But she wondered if it would be Steve and Rachel who would be doing the chaperoning.

* * *

Callie was a bundle of nerves as she got ready for the evening. She changed clothes three times before settling on a simple, but elegant, teal-colored dress. Her hair was also subjected to a variety of styles before she decided to wear it down. She got the perfume right on the first try—slightly spicy, but not overpowering.

The restaurant they went to was casual by New York standards, but it was the closest Harrison came to five-star dining. Callie had been surprised when Rorke had suggested it.

She couldn't remember seeing him wear anything besides blue jeans or coveralls since he'd started high school. But tonight he'd dressed for the occasion. Looking to her right, where he sat next to her at the round table, she indulged herself in the sight of him. Despite his more formal attire he still sent her heart racing. There was no doubt in her mind now—it wasn't just the bad-boy image that kicked her hormones into overdrive, it was Rorke himself.

The kiss they'd shared this afternoon was never far from the front of her mind. And the way Rorke kept dropping his gaze to her lips didn't help.

What would have happened if Steve and Rachel hadn't come home when they had?

She'd been nervous, but Callie knew Rorke would have tried to soothe her, and she knew he would have succeeded. In Rorke's arms, her desires outweighed her fears. It was only when she had time to think about it that she was in charge again and able to make rational decisions.

Dinner passed in a blur. She kept falling into the valley of awareness between herself and Rorke.

Over coffee, Callie and Rachel excused themselves to go to the ladies' room. Rachel didn't say anything about Rorke. But Callie could tell from Rachel's smug, satisfied look that she had picked up on the undercurrents passing between them.

As they stepped out into the hallway and started back to the dining room, a man moved away from the wall and blocked Callie's way.

"Living in the Big Apple hasn't improved your taste in men, has it, Ms. Harrison?"

Callie knew the man had drank more than his share this evening. "Excuse me." She started to walk past him.

"Ten years ago, you lied your way out of it and everyone believed you. Told me I was either blind or lying to get back at you for snubbing me. But how are you going to get out of it this time with so many witnesses?"

Rachel gave Callie's elbow a squeeze before disappearing toward the dining room. Callie hoped she would bring back a member of the staff, but she had a feeling Rachel would return with Rorke.

Callie looked more closely at the man, looked through ten years of his overindulging. "Bradley Peters?" She'd always wondered who'd spread the rumors about her and Rorke.

His smile was feral. "How kind of you to remember. But you didn't answer my question."

"There's nothing to get out of. I'm here having dinner with friends."

"Friends? O'Neil and friends don't belong in the same sentence."

"We're friends, and if you noticed Steve and Rachel—"

"You don't owe him any explanations." Rorke's hands settled onto Callie's shoulders. She leaned back against the security of his chest and wondered how much of the conversation he'd heard.

Bradley glared at Rorke. "You seem to have forgotten your place, O'Neil."

Callie felt Rorke's grip tighten in anger. Before he had a chance to respond, a member of the staff was leading Bradley away. The owner of the restaurant came up, immediately apologizing. Callie was the main focus of his remorse, but he included Steve and Rachel on the periphery, ignoring Rorke.

Rorke didn't say a word, but when Callie snuck a glance at him, she could see his jaw muscles pulled tight. When the four of them returned to the dining room, she deliberately slipped her hand into his.

Looking around the crowded room, she could see Bradley Peters hadn't been the only one to note their presence. She'd been so wrapped up in Rorke earlier, she hadn't noticed.

The censure she saw in their eyes would have intimidated her at eighteen, but now it made her angry. Especially since she knew in their fantasies most of the women would love to be in her shoes, and the men would sell their souls to possess half of Rorke's sex appeal.

They were just having dinner. What would the reaction of the town have been if they had gotten married ten years ago? She couldn't help wondering what

life would be like today if she were Mrs. Rorke O'Neil.
Would they still be together or would they have ended
up divorced? Would they have had children? Would
her father have carried out his threats? Would Rorke
still be working for his father? What would she be
doing?

The rest of the evening appeared to run smoothly,
but Callie could feel the difference. The underlying
awareness between her and Rorke was no longer
flowing freely. He wasn't completely withdrawn, but
he'd moved back.

After the men dropped them off, Callie and Rachel
changed into casual clothes and sat down on opposite
ends of the couch.

"Just think, by this time next week you'll be hon-
eymooning on an island paradise." She tried to sound
cheerful.

"Do you want to talk about what happened at the
restaurant, Callie?" Rachel asked.

She wanted very much to talk about it—with Rorke.
"Not really. I'd rather talk about something pleasant."

"Bradley Peters has always been a jerk. Don't let
him get to you."

But it was more than Bradley. It was the restaurant
owner and the other customers, too.

Ten years ago she had seen Rorke's isolation from
the town and sensed his loneliness. She had reached
out to him, done what she could to ease his solitude.

Tonight she had to reach out again.

Six

———

Rorke looked up at the house, clearly visible in the moonlight. So, he'd forgotten his place, had he? He had news for Bradley Peters and the rest of this town...this *was* his place.

Surely the owner of the second largest house in town had the right to take Calista Harrison to dinner.

Maybe...

For the first time, he began to have doubts about his decision to return to Vermont. Maybe Harrison would always judge him by who he'd been rather than by who he was.

This evening he'd dressed for the occasion...he'd walked into the restaurant with Callie, Steve and Rachel, all considered respectable by the citizens of Harrison...and he'd used the right fork. But he'd felt the silent condemnation of the other patrons and the restaurant staff from the minute he'd sat down. What would they have said if they'd known he'd once had the audacity to ask her to marry him?

Even better—how would they have liked it if her acceptance had been genuine and the two of them had gotten married? Images of them together, possibly with children, flashed into his mind. He quickly turned his thoughts back to the condemnation of the people at the restaurant. It hurt less to think about what had happened this evening than to think about what might have been with Callie.

"You're just spoiled, O'Neil. Too much red-carpet treatment has gone to your head." The places Rorke frequented in New York all knew him as a man with plenty of money in his pockets and treated him with respect. It was an adjustment to be treated like pond scum.

The townspeople's attitudes would change when they found out his position with Yankee. He wished he could be there to see the look on Bradley Peters's face when he heard the news. Daily life would take on a whole different perspective. He would be sought after rather than shunned.

It was what he'd planned to do when he'd walked away—come back with the money and power to buy and sell every last one of the respectable residents of Harrison. In the early years of Yankee he'd outgrown his plot for revenge, but he'd succeeded in accomplishing his original goal anyway. It was a shallow victory at best and far from what he longed for.

The key to the house was in his pocket. Steve and his crew had finished Friday. The decorator was to begin her work on Monday. Everything had already been chosen and ordered. It just needed to be moved in.

He thought about going inside to look around. Instead, he walked to the back of the house. Two steps led up to the patio deck outside the family room door. He sat down on the top step and looked out at the meadow washed in moonlight.

His meadow.

Even before he'd started making plans for moving from New York to Harrison, he'd known this was exactly where he wanted to build.

His father had been surprised when he'd told him he was thinking about returning. He hadn't tried to influence his actions one way or another, but Rorke suspected he liked the idea of the two of them living closer to each other.

Michael O'Neil was a wonderful father and a very wise man. Only now Rorke was beginning to understand how wise.

Years before, when his mother had left them, his father had stoically stepped into his role of single parent and never looked back. Rorke hadn't thought anything of it at the time, being so young and being trapped in his own hell of abandonment, but later when he was twenty and Callie had turned her back on him, he'd realized how much his father must have suffered.

Suffered alone, never letting his son see, doing his best to offer what comfort he could to make an unbearable situation bearable.

In his innocence, Rorke was sure he himself had made his father's burden heavier. Late at night, in the weeks before his mother had left, when he was supposed to be sleeping, he'd heard the arguments about money, and, after her departure, he'd heard the gossip around town. He knew his mother had left them for a rich man.

With the simplified vision of a child, Rorke begged his father to make lots of money so they could "buy Mommy back."

His father gathered him into his arms and let him cry. When the tears slowed and sobs became sniffles, Michael O'Neil sat his son on his knee. "Rorke, the things you buy with money in this life are not the things that will make you happy. Especially people. If you have to buy people, you're better off without them."

If you have to buy people, you're better off without them.

It was true, there was no denying it. There was also no denying that with the Yankee plant he was buying the townspeople of Harrison. And he knew already there would be no happiness in it.

At least he would be able to take Callie out to dinner without being treated like an outcast.

Whoa, put the brakes on. It wasn't likely he'd be taking Callie out again. Whatever developed between them during her visit was temporary.

He couldn't suppress the slow smile as he thought back to this afternoon. People who knew him well would swear he didn't have a vindictive, vengeful bone in his body. But then how else could he explain the sheer glee that had shot through him when he realized Callie was jealous of the woman he'd given a ride to on Friday night?

It didn't matter that other than an evening ride on his motorcycle, there wasn't anything for her to be jealous of. He didn't even know the woman's name, but for all Callie knew, he might have spent the better part of the weekend in the woman's bed. He'd be damned if he'd tell her otherwise.

His smile faded slowly and his jeans grew uncomfortably tight as he thought back on the kiss that had followed her jealous reaction. Damn, it had felt so good holding her, kissing her, touching her, feeling her respond to him in return.

Something distinctive and extraordinary happened when they were in close contact with each other. He was sure even if he had on a blindfold and earplugs, he would be able to pick Callie out of a group of women from that reaction alone. For comfort's sake, he tried to put it out of his mind, but the view before him made matters worse.

He didn't remember everything about all the times he'd made love. But every detail of that long-ago night he'd made love to Callie, here in the meadow, was permanently etched into his memory as clearly as the kiss they'd shared this afternoon. Every detail of that night long ago: every kiss, every word, every sigh.

He'd been her first lover, and on an emotional level she'd been his. His first and his only. Not that he'd deliberately avoided falling in love again—it had just never happened. It was impossible to force it; he should know, he'd tried for years.

He shoved his hands in his jacket pockets, stretching his legs out in front of him, trying to find a more comfortable position. Even the coolness of the night air was having no effect on the tight heat in his lower body as he relived vivid memories.

It was cool tonight, as June nights often were in Vermont. Maybe things would have been different if ten years ago the night hadn't been unseasonably warm. But then again maybe not...

As cool as it was tonight, if Callie were here he'd make love to her. Of course he had hoped to have her in a bed, but if she were here, he didn't think he could wait. The plush carpet in the house crossed his mind, but in the years to come he didn't want Callie's ghost living there with him. It was bad enough she would haunt this meadow forever.

So once more in the meadow it would be. He'd sweep her up into his arms and lay her down beneath the willow tree. Then he'd start on her buttons, opening them one by one, exposing her to his eyes and the filtered moonlight....

The sound of a car coming up the driveway interrupted the erotic play in his mind.

The lights had been out at the garage. Assuming Rorke was asleep, but not ready to go back to Rachel's, Callie drove out to the Yankee owner's house.

Steve said it was finished, so this might be her last chance to visit before the new owner moved in. She grabbed a blanket from her trunk and set off for the meadow.

She glanced briefly at the house towering over her, and wondered again which of the three Yankee owners it belonged to. Once she reached her destination, there was only one man on her mind.

Visions and images of time spent here flooded her senses. She could see Rorke, hear him, feel him and taste him. Or were these memories coming from this afternoon's kiss?

Blanket clutched tightly to her chest, walking slowly, she crossed the meadow.

Callie couldn't bring herself to step through the branches of the willow tree—she just couldn't. It was enough that she was here in the moonlight. She spread out the blanket next to the creek and sat down in the center of it, drawing her knees up and resting her chin on them.

So many memories...she could almost feel Rorke's presence. Strongest were the creak of leather and the scent of his after-shave. The after-shave was definitely a new memory from this afternoon or from dinner. Rorke had been wearing the same one this evening, and although she hadn't gotten as close to him as she had when he'd kissed her, she'd still caught whiffs of the fragrance.

A wave of compassion washed over her. She knew the incident at the restaurant must have hurt him. Would people treat him the same way at the wedding?

She was surprised he was able to sleep. Of course the lights being out over the garage didn't mean he was sleeping.

She pictured him in the dark, alone and hurting. She longed to be there with him, to be there for him. Once he had told her that when she held him, nothing in the world mattered, that no one could say or do anything to hurt him as long as he had her love. She'd taken the comfort away from him, so what good would she be to him now?

A shadow spread over the blanket in front of her. She turned quickly and looked up to see Rorke standing between her and the moon. It had to be Rorke—illusions didn't cast shadows.

He didn't say anything, just stood looking down at her. A tinge of fear crept over her. He had been her friend and lover once, but now he was virtually a stranger.

"I . . . I thought you were sleeping."

"I'm very much awake. Although when I first saw you, I thought I might be dreaming."

"I drove by the garage and the lights were out, so I assumed . . ."

He shoved his hands into his jacket pockets. "Were you looking for me so we could pick up where we left off this afternoon?"

She was immediately aware of how isolated they were, miles from any occupied houses, a good half mile from the road whose nighttime traffic could only be described as sparse.

She felt vulnerable sitting in the middle of a blanket with him towering over her. What if she answered yes to his question? Would he drop down to the blanket with her and pick up where they'd left off? If she said no, would he believe her?

"I thought you might want to talk about what happened this evening at the restaurant."

"Ah, the princess has come to my rescue. If that's why you're here, you may as well leave. I don't need you to fight my battles for me."

Callie stood and moved to stand next to him. "I had no way of knowing you were here. I came here fighting my own battles."

"And what opponents have drawn you to the battlefield this evening, Princess?"

"I don't know exactly. Mostly, I guess, I wanted to say goodbye to the meadow. Since it will belong to someone else soon."

"It's always belonged to someone else."

"The Duncans, I know...I know." She sighed. "But didn't you ever feel like it was ours? Yours and mine?"

He turned his head and looked down at her. The raw emotion on his face caused her to catch her breath. "Yes, I did." It was little more than a whisper.

She looked up at him. Hope surged through her. Would he let her explain about the past now? Was he willing to listen? "I was thinking about the last night I was here."

His withdrawal was immediate and clearly visible even in the subdued light as he returned his gaze to the creek, his shoulders pulled back and tense.

Callie knew she had to change the subject. "What about you? Why are you here?"

For long moments he didn't answer. Just when Callie was convinced he wasn't going to, he said, "Thinking about my decision to move back to Harrison. Wondering if I made a mistake."

"Because of what happened this evening?"

He nodded, burying his hands even deeper into his pockets and rolling his shoulders forward.

Bradley Peters and the rest of the hypocrites better hope they never ran into her in a dark alley. "Rorke, you were born here, too. Harrison is your home as much as it's theirs."

"That may be true, but it's rather idealistic to expect everyone else to believe it, sweetheart."

He was right; she was being idealistic. But it was so unfair. Without stopping to think, she reached out to comfort him. She slipped her arms around his waist, stepped forward and lay her head on his chest. "You're right. But it's not fair."

Slowly he brought his hands out of his pockets and wrapped his arms around her. "Do you know what's even more unfair?"

She shook her head and leaned back to look up at him. Expecting a contemplative expression on his face, she was stunned by his wicked smile and the glimmer of mischief in his eyes.

"What is unfair, Ms. Harrison, is that I'm wasting time talking about something I can't change while standing with a beautiful woman in my arms."

Her heartbeat picked up speed and she felt a warm awareness of the man holding her. "Well...what would you rather talk about?"

He reached up and ran one strong hand down the side of her face until he nestled it under her jaw, tilting her head back. "We could talk about how your skin glows in the moonlight." Moving his hand lower, he kept his gaze locked with hers. "And speculate whether it's just your face, or if the rest of your skin would be as lovely."

Callie sucked in her breath as his touch continued downward over the swell of one breast—both felt suddenly heavy and her nipples tingled as they began to tighten and push against the lace of her bra.

She wanted his hand to linger, to explore. Instead it continued down, slipping along the curve of her waist, then around to the small of her back. Using both hands now, Rorke pulled her into the cradle of his thighs, rocking her gently against him. "Or we could speculate about how much pressure denim can handle."

Callie could feel the extent of the pressure his blue jeans were being called upon to contain.

"Or maybe we shouldn't talk at all."

Before Callie could think of a response, Rorke had leaned down and covered her mouth with his. The kiss was not the sweet, gentle coaxing of this afternoon— it was hot, wild and hungry. Bursting open the door within her and pulling her across the threshold in an uncontrollable rush.

Her hands clutched convulsively at the cool leather covering his back. She wanted to feel warm skin beneath her fingertips. The noise she made deep in her throat was part pleasure and part frustration.

Rorke pulled back, his breathing shallow and irregular. "I know, baby, I know." He cupped her face between his hands and traced her bottom lip with his thumbs. "It's not enough, is it?"

He looked over at the willow tree, then down at the blanket spread out a few feet from them. Sweeping her up in his arms, he carried her to the blanket. After laying her down, he took off her tennis shoes and then his boots before joining her.

Stretched out on his side, he ran his finger down the center of her sweatshirt. "No buttons."

"Buttons?"

"Before you arrived, I was thinking about making love to you. You were wearing the dress you wore to dinner and I had to undo the buttons to get to what was underneath."

She'd known what they were doing on the blanket—or more precisely what they *would* be doing—but actually hearing Rorke say the words *making love* made it seem more real. The fantasy, the illusion of old memories and his sudden appearance faded beneath the solid facts of the aching needs of her body and the ability of the man beside her to fill those needs.

"I would have left it on if I'd known."

"Don't worry. My interest is not on your wardrobe, but what's underneath." He moved closer to her and with cooperation was able to slip her sweatshirt off.

He continued to undress her, and she in turn worked at removing his clothes. Before she slipped his jeans down, he pulled a foil packet out of his pocket and dropped it onto the blanket.

She'd carried a memory of a gorgeous male body with broad shoulders and lean hips. But the body she uncovered was breathtaking. There was more muscle definition in his powerful male torso and the patterns of dark hair on his chest had expanded and grown thicker over the years.

Ten years ago she'd been too timid to do more than glance at him through half-lowered lashes. Now she couldn't tear her gaze away. He was gloriously male. The sight of him, naked with the silver light of the moon highlighting and casting shadows, sent shock waves of desire through her.

Looking up, she found him watching her. He smiled, an invitation, and reached out to her.

Callie moved into his arms. Her mind was flooded with things she wanted to tell him: how good it felt...how much she'd missed him...how much she'd loved him and how much she suspected she still did. The feeling was stronger now than it had ever been. Instead of telling him in words, she leaned forward and kissed him.

He opened his mouth under hers, and she accepted that invitation, too. She moved gently against him, teasing her nipples through the rough hairs on his chest.

The cool night air, sweeping over skin that was not pressed tightly to Rorke's heat, was enough of a distraction to leave her a scrap of control. Instead of pushing it away, she grabbed on to it frantically, hanging on for dear life.

Maybe if she could stay in control, she could loosen the past's hold on her, truly put it to rest and not just bury it alive where it could come out to haunt her. If she could replace the memories of overwhelming ecstasy with a pleasant, but tamer joining, perhaps she could finally get on with her life without Rorke shadowing her relationships.

It was a narrow ledge of control she was perched on, but maybe it would be enough.

She almost lost her battle when Rorke moved over her and into her in one long, smooth motion. But she focused on feeling his heartbeat behind the hard wall of his chest and trailing her hands over his shoulders and down his back.

She looked over his shoulder, up to the sky. Only the brightest stars were visible, since the moon shone in full brilliance.

She started to slip again when Rorke moved his hands beneath her hips and pressed more tightly into her. Maybe she could count the stars.

Rorke swore and pulled back until his body was no longer joined to hers, but he was still close—so close she could feel the heat of his arousal.

She looked up at him, her eyes wide with surprise at his withdrawal. Her puzzlement doubled when she saw what the effort was costing him. Why was he denying himself something he so obviously wanted?

"Do you want me to stop?" His voice was tight and strained.

"I . . ." *Did she?*

"Callie, I'm not going to let you cheat me or you. But I'll stop if you want me to."

"No, I don't want you to." It was the truth. She didn't want him to stop. She wanted the togetherness of making love with him. She just didn't want the vulnerability of complete surrender.

"You're sure?"

"I'm sure." She ran her hands up the tight columns of his arms.

"If we're going to do it, we're going to do it right and we're going to do it together."

His words left no room for compromise and neither did his actions. Supporting himself with one arm, he moved his other hand between them. Placing his open palm flat just below her navel, he slowly slid it lower. As his fingers reached their target, he brought his mouth down over the peak of one breast and suckled gently.

Callie gasped and felt the last remnant of her control slip away. She moaned when she realized her hands were raking through Rorke's hair and she didn't remember moving them.

The muscles of her lower belly and inner thighs began to quiver and a swirling emptiness opened within her. Before she could think how to fill it, her body took over. Her hips shifted, then arched up to reclaim what Rorke had been withholding.

"Yes, sweetheart, that's it." His encouragement was a harsh growl against her neck, as he leaned more of his weight onto her, driving forward and pulling back with the force and the rhythm her body defined.

There was a twinge of regret that control had eluded her, but it was quickly driven away by the intimate ecstasy of being one with Rorke.

All the words she'd wanted to say to him earlier tumbled out in incomprehensible gasps and moans.

The emptiness within her was full, full and warm. But as they continued, it became tight and hot. She could feel Rorke's heart beating faster against her own and sense the urgency building within him.

Release, when it came to them both, was strong and wrenching. The waves rocked through Callie's entire body, before subsiding into quivering flutters where she held Rorke within her.

He raised up slightly until he could look in her eyes. The flutters slowed into a peaceful fluidness. Neither of them spoke out loud, but together they marveled at the perfection they had just experienced.

He lowered his head toward her and softly kissed her love-swollen mouth. Rolling over on his back, pulling the blanket around them as he went, he settled her on top of him, gently guiding her head down until it rested on his chest.

Only the sound of the creek broke the silence surrounding them as they lay locked in each other's arms.

"We could have had paradise."

Callie chuckled. "I thought we just did." She raised up and the laughter died in her throat. The joy and wonder had faded from his eyes, leaving behind a sad emptiness.

"We could have had it forever, Callie."

Seven

Forever with Rorke...it sounded wonderful.

He could move back to New York with her, go back to the job he'd left. Her father would probably never find out. If he did, chances were that since he'd disowned her he wouldn't carry through on his threats anyway. But even if he tried, she would be able to fight back. She was older and wiser, had her own financial resources and friends in the legal profession.

"We can have it forever."

Rorke sat up, moving her off him. "No, Callie, we can't." Standing, he walked over to his abandoned jeans.

Callie wrapped the blanket around herself and tried to think of what to say to get the warmth back between them. "I love you, Rorke."

His back was to her as he pulled on his jeans, so she couldn't see his face. But she could hear the ice in his voice. "Don't read more into this than there is."

"Maybe you should tell me what exactly you think there is here."

"A man and a woman who are physically attracted to each other, acting on their sexual drives."

She couldn't have been more astounded it he'd dumped her into the cold water of the creek. "Sexual drives? It was much more than that for me."

Rorke turned toward her, dragging his hands through his hair. Callie watched the play of muscles across his bared chest. "You felt that way in the afterglow last time, too, but we both know how long it lasted."

"It *never* ended, Rorke. That's not why—"

"It doesn't matter why. Why doesn't change the fact that you left me. Knowing why you left wouldn't guarantee that you won't run off and leave me again." He looked at her, his expression grim. "The bottom line here is a matter of trust. I don't trust you, Princess. Unfortunately, that doesn't stop me from wanting you physically. Believe me I wish it did. Since it doesn't, I'll keep a nice warm spot in my bed for you, but that's all I'm willing to risk."

A nice warm spot in his bed? Did he want an open-ended affair? A few hot stolen moments whenever she happened to be in the neighborhood? "I told you I love you. Doesn't that mean anything?"

"Without trust, the phrase 'I love you' is just three empty words."

"You honestly think this was nothing more than sex drives?" Despite the blanket, she was suddenly cold.

She got up and started gathering and separating the articles of clothing they'd scattered earlier, slipping into her own as she found them, throwing Rorke's into a pile next to him. "What about caring and compassion?"

"What about it?" He reached down to pick up his shirt.

"I care about you, Rorke. This evening at the restaurant—"

He dropped his shirt, crossed the two steps between them and grabbed her upper arms. "Now the truth comes out. Pity. That's what this was really about for you, wasn't it? Pity? You felt sorry for me, so you figured I'd feel better if you let me—"

Callie gasped. She was familiar with the expression he'd used, but would never have associated it with the intensely personal lovemaking she and Rorke had shared.

He released her suddenly as though he couldn't bear to touch her. "Damn it, I don't need your pity." He snatched up his shirt and boots. Long angry strides carried him from her.

Callie watched him walk away, her thoughts and emotions jumbled together in an unsortable tangle. It took a major effort to keep from chasing after him, but in the mood he was in she knew there would be no reasoning with him. He needed space and time.

Rorke turned the corner at the side of the house and disappeared from sight. Emptiness opened up in her again, this time around her heart. There was a long pause and she assumed he was putting on the rest of his clothes. A motorcycle engine roared to life, then faded into the distance.

She didn't pity him. There was a big difference between pity and what she felt for Rorke. Caring deeply, compassionately, wasn't the same as pity.

Tonight had felt like a new beginning. The strength of the love she had discovered she still felt for him had astonished her. She had taken it for granted he was feeling the same way.

She finished dressing, then said a silent goodbye to the meadow. Even if it wasn't soon to be someone else's backyard, she didn't think she would ever want to see it again.

There was a not unpleasant soreness between her thighs as she gathered up the blanket and headed back to her car. She didn't regret what had happened, she just didn't want it to be over or reduced to nothing more than sexual drives.

Maybe the old saying about opportunity knocking once was true. Maybe she'd had her chance with Rorke, thrown it away and couldn't have another. The agony was almost more than she could bear. She doubted the ability of time to dull it for her again.

Rorke turned onto Jackson Road, heading away from town. The last thing he wanted from Calista Harrison was pity or sympathy. But that was the least of his problems.

He'd been a fool! How could he have imagined he would be able to make love to her for physical pleasure only?

He should have realized feeding his senses with her would stir up the ashes of his love and the pain he'd felt when she'd left him. Left him for money, he amended.

As he roared down roads he'd haunted in his youth, he let his thoughts wander in the past. The happiness Callie's friendship had brought to his days. The elation he'd felt when her acceptance of his proposal had convinced him that happiness was to be his for the rest of his life.

He relived the day he'd waited in the cold of the morning, his wallet full of cash, his heart full of hopes and dreams.

While he'd waited, he'd gathered wildflowers in the meadow for a wedding bouquet. A bouquet for a wedding that wasn't to be.

As he remembered the details, he felt the emotions—the excitement, the anticipation, the first niggling of impatience, the fear that something might be wrong, the agitation of the frantic rush to Harrison Manor, the anger and despair that followed her father's revelations.

"Don't do this, pal. Don't think about it anymore. It's history. Let it go."

But how could he let it go? After so recently having held Callie in his arms, buried himself in her warmth and felt her yield to the passion between them again. How could he let it go when the events of the past hour had driven home the reality of how much he had lost?

Rachel was up when Callie got back. She knew it would be futile to lie to her friend, but she did no more than admit things had gone wrong between her and Rorke. Luckily Rachel didn't pry any deeper and promised to give up her matchmaking ambitions.

Callie stayed calm by assuring herself this was only a temporary condition. It couldn't really be over. She couldn't let it be over. There had to be a way for her to make him trust her again. But where to start? How could trust be repaired?

Yes, she'd hurt him. It had hurt her to hurt him. She didn't intend to put either of them through it again. How could she make him believe that?

It was a question she asked herself many times during the days that followed. But she couldn't find an answer.

Trusting someone was a leap of faith, and even if she camped out on his doorstep from now until the end of time, Rorke could still refuse to believe she would never leave him again.

Thursday after work, Rorke went upstairs to finish packing his personal items. By this time tomorrow, he would be moving into his new home.

His mind wasn't on what he was doing, or on the house. Despite his best efforts, once again, he was thinking of Callie.

"Moving day?"

Rorke looked up to find his father standing in the doorway.

"Not until tomorrow, but I thought I'd get this out of the way. Alex and Jesse are coming to see the plant around noon, and the wedding rehearsal is tomorrow night...."

"Excited about your nice new house?"

"Sure, Dad." *Not as much as I was before last Sunday.* "You know my offer to build you a house is still open."

Michael shook his head. "I like living over the garage. If I didn't, I would have moved years ago. To my mind, there's no greater luxury than being able to get up in the morning and walk downstairs and be at work. Beats fighting the elements."

"But don't you ever wish you had more space?"

"Son, I'm happy here. And aside from being healthy, there's no greater joy in life than being happy."

"You don't think you would be just as happy in a bigger house?"

Michael laughed. "Big houses don't guarantee happiness. Just look at old man Harrison. He's got the biggest house in town, and he's alone and bitter."

"You two went to high school together. How can you call him old?"

"Because he is. He's old before his time. His big house can't make up for the fact that he hasn't spoken to his own daughter in ten years."

Rorke stopped packing and looked up. "He what?"

"He disowned his only child."

"Callie?" Ten years? Could there be any connection between what he'd just learned and what had gone on between them ten years ago?

"As far as I know, that's the only child he's got."

"What happened?"

"No one knows for sure. All we know is that he changed his will. He's leaving everything to his oldest nephew."

"But you don't know why?"

"No one seems to know the reason. I figured you knew all about it though, the two of you being friends and all."

For the second time since his father'd shown up, Rorke was stunned. "How did you know?"

"I'd have to be blind and deaf not to. She'd drive by, and within ten minutes you'd be wheeling out of here."

Rorke rubbed the back of his neck where angry muscles screamed with tension.

If Mr. Harrison had paid Callie's college bills in exchange for her giving him up, as he'd claimed when Rorke had confronted him, then why had he disowned her? Did her father consider her completely ruined because she'd been with him? He knew Mr. Harrison didn't like him, but could he hate him that much? Something wasn't adding up. Hell, *nothing* was adding up!

"I need to talk to her."

"Are you all right, son?"

"I need to talk to Callie." But would she agree to talk to him? "Damn, I wish the house was ready."

"What's the house got to do with it?"

"She's staying with Rachel and I need to talk to her alone."

"Did I mention I was going over to Exeter to play a little cards with Joe and the guys? Won't be back 'til morning."

"I thought you played on Friday nights."

"We're playing on Thursday this week. Sam's anniversary is tomorrow night."

"And since when did you play all night long?"

"Didn't I teach you not to look a gift horse in the mouth, son?" He walked over to the dresser, picked up the key ring sitting there, tossed it to Rorke and turned to leave. "Good luck," he said over his shoulder.

* * *

Callie was finishing their after-dinner cleanup and Rachel was at the kitchen table writing thank-you notes for shower gifts, when Callie thought she heard the roar of a motorcycle engine. It was a deep-pitched grumbling, the double thumping heartbeat of a V-twin engine, rather than a high-pitched whine, but it didn't sound like the Indian.

"Callie, is it Rorke?"

Callie shrugged. "I don't know."

They walked into the living room and looked out the front window. The motorcycle parked in Rachel's driveway was an exceptional piece of machinery and work of art rolled into one. White pearlescent paint and sparkling chrome glinted in what was left of the day's sunlight, but Callie had little time to appreciate it before her attention was grabbed by the rider coming up the front walkway.

She clasped her arms around her waist, trying to ward off the shivers of awareness she knew were coming.

"Do you want to talk to him?" Rachel asked.

"Do I have a choice?"

"I could tell him you're not here."

"My car's right out front."

"I can maneuver my way around that." The doorbell rang. "Well?"

"I'll talk to him." She tried to stay calm while Rachel answered the door and she heard Rorke ask for her, but it was impossible. Her future happiness was on the line and she was a bundle of nerves.

Rachel stepped back and Callie walked to the door. Her gaze focused on the ground, she stopped when she saw dusty black leather.

"Hello, Callie."

She bit the inside of her lip and forced herself to look up. "Rorke." From the confused play of emotions in his eyes, it seemed this was as hard on him as it was on her. "Nice bike."

He glanced over his shoulder. "Thanks, I'm rather attached to it."

"I take it that's your Yankee?"

"Yep." He stuffed his hands into the pockets of his blue jeans. "Would you like to go for a ride?"

The words *anywhere and anytime* threatened to burst out, but the memory of his offer of a warm spot in his bed, held them back. "I don't think I'd better. You see, I'm not a one-night stand, Rorke. Although that's essentially what happened the other night. I didn't recognize it for what it was until after it was over."

"Ouch." One strong, tanned hand came up to rub the back of his neck. "I suppose I deserved that." He reached out and took her hand, twining his fingers with hers. "I'm sorry for most of what I said the other night."

"Most?"

He flashed her a wicked smile. "You wouldn't want me to take back things like how beautiful your skin looks in the moonlight and how warm and—"

Callie glanced over her shoulder and was glad to see no sign of Rachel. "Apology accepted."

"Good. So what do you say, want a ride?"

She still wasn't sure his offer wasn't an offer of sex. "Rorke, I don't think it's a very good idea."

"Callie, we need to talk."

She started to move back. "Let's go into the kitchen then."

"Alone."

There was a pleading, almost desperate look in his eyes. "Where?" She couldn't face the meadow again.

"My father's gone out for the evening. I thought we could talk at his place. This is not a plot to get you in bed, Callie."

Maybe she could help restore his trust in her by demonstrating her trust in him. "All right. Let me tell Rachel I'm leaving."

"Thank you." He squeezed her hand gently before letting her go.

A few minutes later, she was walking out the front door. She noticed several of the neighbors sitting on their front porches staring openly. At other houses, curtains were not hanging as straight as they should have been.

Once they both had helmets on and Rorke was seated on the bike, she got on behind him. Aware of the many eyes watching, she scooted way forward, leaning into him willingly, pressing intimately against him from shoulder to knee . . . no need for the coaxing there had been the other night. Fuel for the rumor mill, and exquisite torture for her body. She hoped Rorke wasn't getting the wrong idea.

By the time they reached their destination, she was so physically aroused, a warm spot in his bed sounded incredibly appealing.

"So, what do you think of the bike?"

"Nice, smooth ride." *As far as the machinery is concerned.* It suddenly occurred to her, she hadn't dreamed about the man in the Yankee ad since before last Sunday night. "Is it a Yankee Spirit, Yankee Clipper or Yankee Pride?"

"None of the above." He ran his hand over the curve of the handlebar. "It's a custom model. One of a kind."

After closing up the garage, he led her upstairs.

Callie had been in the apartment on several occasions in the past and was amazed at the changes. It had always seemed impossibly neat and tidy for the home of two bachelors, but now its comfortable homey atmosphere seemed to have a decorator's touch.

"New furniture?"

"It's been ten years." Pain, confusion and regret were all present in his eyes. "Would you like something to drink? Soda, ice tea, coffee?"

"No, thanks, not right now."

"Why don't we sit down, then."

Callie sat on one end of the couch. Rorke sat in the recliner to her right, leaning forward with his arms resting on his thighs and his hands clasped between his knees.

She was expecting him to bring up the subject of last Sunday night and was surprised when he brought up her father.

"I don't think it's a big secret in town that my father disowned me," she answered.

"Apparently not, but I haven't been around and I've never been a regular link in the gossip chain. Just one of their favorite subjects. I didn't hear about you and your father until today."

Callie shrugged. "Well, it's true."

"I hear it happened about ten years ago."

She nodded.

"Is that why you left town?"

"No, he didn't disown me until the end of the year. He'd wanted me to come home over Christmas vacation, and I told him not only would I not come home for the holiday, but I would never set foot in his house again."

"I'm surprised he didn't cut off your college money... or did you get it in a lump sum?"

"My father couldn't cut off my college money. It was in a trust fund set up by my mother's father."

"But he controlled it, right?"

"No. It was mine the day I graduated from high school. Why?"

He was on his feet, disbelief and anger battling for control of his features. "Did you or did you not convince your father to pay your college bills in exchange for leaving me?"

Callie felt the blood drain from her face. "Where did you get such an idea?"

"Your father."

"My father?"

"Remember, I told you I went over there when you didn't show up."

She nodded. He'd told her about it the day they'd formed their truce.

"He told me you'd come to him and said that unless he agreed to pay your way at whatever college you chose, you would marry me. But it was a lie, wasn't it? I can see it on your face." He sunk back down to the chair. "Damn it, it was all a lie." He dropped his head into his hands.

Callie wasn't surprised her father had lied to Rorke. Turning Rorke against her was one more guarantee that he would get his way. She had a few choice words she'd like to say to him, but most important at the moment was doing something for Rorke's pain.

She went over to him, going down on her knees and leaning forward against his legs. He moved his hands down to frame her face. She had never seen such anguish as she saw in his eyes.

"You didn't desert me for money, did you?"

"No."

He took a deep breath, and released it slowly. "Did you really love me?"

"With all my heart."

A choking sound broke from his throat. He wrapped his arms around her. Opening his knees and moving forward, he pulled her tightly against him. Burying his head on her shoulder, he repeated her name over and over in a harsh gasping voice.

In turn, Callie held him just as tightly. Tears gathered in her eyes as she thought about how much worse her leaving must have hurt him if he'd thought she'd left him for money.

"Then why, Callie, why? Why was I good enough to give your virginity to, but not good enough to marry?"

"I wanted to marry you." She pulled back so they could look at each other. His arms still wrapped around her, her hands resting on his chest.

"What stopped you?"

"My father came into my room while I was packing. I . . . I tried to tell him I was going to spend the night at Rachel's. Even though it was the first time I'd ever lied to him, he didn't believe me. Apparently he'd heard the rumors that I'd been seen with you and he kept after me until finally I told him the truth . . . that I loved you and we were leaving in the morning to get married."

"I'll bet that made his day."

"I've never seen him so angry." Her hands clenched into tight fists. "He ranted and raved, and when it was all said and done, the bottom line was that if I married you he would use his power and influence to destroy us financially and by reputation. And not just us, but your father and any children we had."

Rorke was staring at the far wall, looking as thunderous as her father had that night so many years ago. "That bastard. I hope he rots in hell." He turned and looked down at her. "Why didn't you come and tell me about this when it happened? Maybe we could have done something, at least left town together."

"Your father would have been left behind. It wouldn't have been fair for him to lose everything your family had worked for in Harrison."

Rorke shrugged. "He might have been willing to leave with us."

"Maybe. But back then I believed my father was so powerful, he could destroy us even if we weren't in town. I didn't realize he was just a big fish in a little pond, and by moving away we could have found bigger fish who would have been on our side." She sighed. "What I kept seeing vividly in my mind, was you losing your temper and storming off to Harrison Manor. With the mood my father was in, I knew he would slap you with an assault charge if you so much as brushed against him.''

Rorke nodded. ''I probably would have been tempted to have a few words with him before we left.''

''A few words?''

''Figure of speech. At twenty I would have 'brushed against him'... forcefully. But if you'd asked me not to, I probably wouldn't have gone to see him at all.''

''I can't go back and do things differently. That night I felt so alone. Maybe if my mother had still been alive... If she'd been there for me to talk to I might have been able to think of other options. All I could see was that the two of you would be safe if I left.'' She leaned forward, resting her forehead against his chest. ''Rorke, I'm sorry. So very sorry.''

He reached down and gathered her up. Scooting back in the chair he arranged her in his lap, cuddling her head against his shoulder.

''You did what you thought you had to do. If I'd been in your shoes, I might have made the same choice.'' He ran his hand along the curve of her cheek. ''And if I'd known he'd lied to me about your money, threats or no threats, I *would* have come after you.''

''I wondered sometimes if you would come for me. When you didn't, I convinced myself you didn't really love me.''

''I loved you so damn much. But I bought your father's explanation, and since I believed you didn't love me, my pride wouldn't let me chase after you.''

''You never suspected he might have lied?''

''No. I kept thinking about that old song about wanting a girl like the girl that married dear old Dad, and I figured I'd found one.''

Callie turned in his lap to reach her arms around his neck and hold him close. Their youthful relationship seemed tarnished by Rorke's seemingly easy acceptance of her father's lies. Then again, she'd gotten through the past ten years by believing Rorke hadn't really loved her, had only been trying to add a notch to his belt. She knew better now.

Hadn't the fact that he'd been her first lover shown how deeply she felt about him? "But I'd let you make love to me. Didn't that prove I loved you?"

He shrugged. "I thought maybe you'd planned it as an act of rebellion against your father."

"I didn't plan it. I wouldn't have known *how*. I was always shy about the subject of sex. Actually, when I first heard about it, I couldn't believe people would really do such a thing. But then that night in the meadow...the moonlight...the brook..."

"I still remember every detail, too."

"It was magic, Rorke. I wasn't as embarrassed as I'd expected to be the first time, but I was a bit scared."

"It was scary, wasn't it?"

"For me. Surely not for you."

"Yes. For me, too. I knew it was your first time, and I wanted to go slowly so it would be perfect. But damn, sweetheart, you'd just agreed to marry me and I wanted you so much."

She leaned back slightly, until she could look at him. "I wanted you, too."

"I know. That made it even harder to keep things slow and easy. It had been a while since I'd made love. From the first day I'd kissed you, I couldn't stand the thought of touching another woman."

"But that was several months."

"I know. And at that stage of my life it was the longest stretch my hormones had ever had to wait, and the night in the meadow they took over. Maybe I should have waited. Things might have been different if I'd waited."

"So many ifs, Rorke."

The last of the anger faded from his eyes, leaving sad resignation behind. "*Too* many ifs." He leaned his head back, closing his eyes.

How could she have done this to him? She hugged him and buried her face against his shoulder. "I can't tell you how sorry I am." Tears escaped her eyes to fall on the soft fabric of his shirt.

"Sweetheart, it's not your fault."

"If only I'd talked to you, told you why I was leaving..."

"Don't forget you were eighteen years old. A very sheltered, innocent eighteen."

"I don't think I can ever forgive myself."

One large hand cradled her head, the other made soothing circles on her back. "I forgive you." He leaned forward, turned her in his arms and moved his mouth over hers in a sweet kiss to heal old wounds.

He forgave her. It meant so much to have his forgiveness. And at least now she fully understood why he could never trust her.

Callie was having trouble breathing by the time he broke the kiss. Her pulse was racing and she felt herself slipping under his sensual spell.

She moved her hand up to curve around his neck and thread through the ends of his hair. It felt so good sitting securely in his lap.

"What about the issue of trust, Rorke?" She hated to ruin the moment, but the question had to be asked. "Can you trust me now?"

A shadow settled in his eyes. "That's a hard question. Right now at this moment, I can't answer because I don't know you. It's been ten years...."

She'd wanted a declaration of love and trust. His answer was a disappointment, but she could see his point and realized, despite the love she felt for him in her heart, she didn't know the man he was today any more than he knew the woman she was. "So where does that leave us?"

Eight

Rorke's arms tightened around her and his gaze dropped to her lips. A look with so much longing, she could almost feel it.

This time she was the one who started the kiss.

When she slipped her hands between them to loosen the buttons of his shirt, he stopped her. Getting to his feet, still holding her, he carried her into his bedroom.

The double bed taking up most of the room looked inviting, but his father could return at any moment.

"Rorke, we can't."

"Why? Why can't we?" He placed several soft kisses on each side of her mouth before he pulled back to give her a chance to answer.

"I guess we can, but we shouldn't."

"Is there someone else? Some man waiting patiently for you in New York?"

She laughed. "This is a fine time to ask."

"I take it that's a no."

"No, there's no man in New York. But what about your father?"

"He won't be back until morning."

"What about my father?"

"I don't think we need to worry about him at this point. But if the time comes when we do, I'll take care of things."

"But—"

"Trust me."

Once again she wondered if by demonstrating her trust, she could help him come to trust her. "All right."

He slowly set her on her feet, but kept her close. "So what do you say, wanna have a slumber party?"

She tilted her head to one side and looked up at him with love-softened eyes. "Only if you don't let me get too much sleep."

"That's going to be an easy promise to keep."

Clothes were a simple obstacle to deal with after all the other barriers they'd crashed through over the course of the evening.

"It feels strange doing this inside for a change," Callie said as Rorke pulled her down onto the bed.

"We could go out in the backyard if you'd like."

She rested her head on the cool pillow slip. "No, this will be fine."

"Callie, love, I have dreamed this a million times. Lying in bed with you beside me."

"Me, too."

He reached out and drew her to him, aligning their bodies, soft inviting curves to hard aggressive muscle. His hands moved down to pull her hips forward, pressing her lower body even more snugly against his. She arched against him.

Leaning forward, he placed heated kisses on the smooth curve of her neck, then slowly slid down until he could take an already aroused nipple into his mouth.

He had been a skilled lover at twenty, but now he was an artist. And the knowledge that he forgave her youthful mistake added to the delight she found in his arms.

They came together lighthearted and playful, but soon laughter gave way to gasps and they both were lost to everything except the instincts that drove them toward a shattering climax.

Rorke rested his head on the pillow next to her. Using one tan finger, he turned her head to look at him. He kissed her gently. She fought to hold back a yawn.

"I think you're ready for a nap."

"I think you're right. I haven't been sleeping well lately."

Rorke got up, flipped the lights off and went into the living room to do the same thing.

Moonlight spilled in across the darkness. Callie sat up and looked out the window. She could see the outline of hills against the horizon and Harrison Manor on one of them. The outdoor lighting lit up the structure assisted by the occasional illuminated window.

She heard Rorke reenter the room. "You can see Harrison Manor from your bedroom window."

"Couldn't you see the garage from yours?"

"Yes, but I guess I never stopped to consider it worked both ways." She looked over at him. "How do you know which room was mine?"

He sat down next to her and gathered her into his arms. "The night I fixed your tire, I watched you drive up the hill to the house and then waited to see which light went on. Second floor, second window from the right."

"You know, lit up that way and from this angle, it really does look like a castle."

"You should see it in winter, with the snow glittering in the moonlight." His arms tightened. "I was so convinced it was a castle that when my mother began telling me bedtime stories about an unhappy princess waiting for a knight to rescue her, I was sure she was talking about you. I couldn't figure out why you never looked unhappy when I saw you."

His voice took on a melancholy note. "But she wasn't talking about you at all. Many years later, I realized she was talking about herself. Her knight was already in sight, she just hadn't brought him to heel yet."

One of the things he'd talked about when they'd been together before was his plan to someday track his mother down. "Did you ever try to find her?"

"She saved me the trouble. She looked me up a few years ago."

"How was it?"

"It was hard." Callie could feel the tenseness in his muscles. "She still puts a greater value on money than on people. I'll never understand people like that." He placed a kiss on top of her head.

It was the last thing Callie remembered before drifting off to sleep.

Rorke woke at sunrise. *Damn, he felt drained.* He was momentarily confused and disoriented. Had he been drinking? Pictures flashed through his mind. He must have been dreaming of Callie.

Again . . . would he ever be over her?

A warm, very female body was curled up against him. He tried to remember who she was, where he'd met her and where they were.

He opened his eyes to the dim morning light. His room at his father's? He looked down at the woman in his arms and came fully awake and fully aware of everything from the night before. Callie . . . she was really here.

They needed to talk before he took her back to Rachel's. He needed to tell her about Yankee Motorworks.

She'd surrendered herself to him not knowing about his money. He would never be able to verbalize how much it meant to him, knowing it was him and him alone she had responded to. Who he was, not what he had or what he could afford to give her.

A shudder ripped through him. Callie made a soft purring sound and slowly opened her eyes. She smiled up at him.

He needed to tell her how money and success hadn't fulfilled him, tell her how empty he'd been. But could he get the words out?

At the moment his throat was tight with emotional intensity and his hands trembled with the need to touch her, the need to feel her respond to him. Despite the countless times they had awaken to make love during the night, he needed to bury himself in her, to feel her accept him yet again and take pleasure from their union.

There would be time later to tell her he now owned Duncan's Woods and their meadow. Tell her she really could be queen in the motorcycle millionaire's castle.

After a fast shower and quick breakfast, Rorke rode Callie back to Rachel's.

Callie got off the motorcycle first. Still straddling the bike, Rorke looked over his shoulder at the houses across the street. "We have an audience again."

"Shall we give them something to talk about?"

"Callie, don't you think the fact that we left here around sunset and didn't return until this morning is enough?"

She cocked her head to one side. "If you don't want to kiss me, just say so."

"But I do want to kiss you."

"Well, then?" She closed the space between them, reaching up to put her arms around his neck.

"Your reputation is in deep trouble, sweetheart."

"Will you hurry up and kiss me already."

Rorke laughed. "You put it so sweetly. How can I refuse?"

By the time Rorke pulled back, they were both breathless. "That's enough for now or we'll have trouble with the law as well as gossiping neighbors."

He got off the bike and walked her to the front door, his arm possessively around her waist.

"I'm going to miss you today."

"I'll see you tonight at the rehearsal."

With one more quick kiss, he left her standing in the doorway. She stood watching until he roared off down the street.

"Guess I don't have to ask how your evening went."

Callie turned to find Rachel sitting on the couch. "Good morning."

"When you manage to come down off the cloud you're floating on, maybe you'd like to tell me about it."

Callie closed the front door and walked over to sit next to Rachel. "I may be moving back to Harrison, after all."

"Great! When?"

"I don't know yet." Callie realized Rorke had never answered her when she'd asked where they went from here. The desire between them had flared up and became the focus of the rest of their time together. She didn't know if they'd be moving in together, having a long-distance affair or if there was a wedding in their future. "We haven't discussed any details, but I think we'll have to do something. Rorke may want to move back to New York, but since he's only recently returned to Harrison...and as you mentioned the other day, I can work free-lance from here...and I'd rather raise my children in Harrison than New York."

Rachel chuckled. "That good, huh?"

"Guess I'm babbling."

"A bit, but it's good to see you so happy."

Callie was still walking on air later that morning when she stopped by the jeweler's to pick up the wedding rings. She had originally planned to give Rachel's ring to Rorke that evening at the rehearsal, but since it was almost lunchtime . . .

Michael O'Neil walked up to the driver's side window when she pulled into the garage parking lot.

"You just missed him. He's on his way to the construction site."

Callie didn't question Mr. O'Neil's accurate assumption that she was there to see Rorke. Looking down the road, she could see him stopped at a stop sign. As she watched he began to move forward.

"I'll catch up with him. Thanks." She waved goodbye to Michael and headed after Rorke.

At the stop sign a car turned from the side street and continued down the road in the direction she was heading. Luckily she could still see Rorke up ahead.

She wondered why he was going out to the construction site. Hadn't Steve said he was finished with the house? She was surprised when Rorke rode past the turnoff to the house. Could Michael have meant the motorcycle plant construction site?

Why would Rorke be going there? Maybe he was taking her suggestion and applying for a job.

She was frustrated by the leisurely pace of the driver in front of her—a pace that allowed Rorke to get farther and farther ahead.

Fortunately the new plant sat on a straight stretch of road and she was able to see him turn into the driveway. She continued to follow.

For a while she didn't think she was going to make it past the security guard manning the gate, but then he recognized her and she explained about the rings for the wedding.

The guard held a clipboard in his hand as he leaned in her car window to talk. It was a list of names and Rorke's was on it.

When she finally made it into the parking lot, she located Rorke's motorcycle sitting in one of the reserved parking spots nearest the walkway that led up to the main entrance. But there was no sign of him.

Callie shook her head and laughed. It was just like him to defy the Reserved Parking sign. She knew he would never ignore a fire lane or handicapped parking, but any other spot would be fair game for him.

She hoped whomever the space was intended for didn't arrive while Rorke was there. She would hate for him to jeopardize his chances for a job over something so trivial as parking in the wrong place. There was a low-slung sports car parked in one of the other reserved spots. The third was empty.

Parking in the next row, facing Rorke's bike, Callie looked around. Stretching across the front, and connecting the large concrete buildings was a chrome-and-tinted-glass structure, which she assumed was the office area of the plant. Landscaping crews were at work on the outside, and an assortment of potted trees were being unloaded from a truck pulled up to the curb, and disappearing one by one through the sliding glass doors into the building.

As she watched, a man in a suit came out the doors and walked over to one of the landscapers. He looked familiar, but she couldn't think of his name. Strange... over the last few weeks she'd been able to remember everyone else's name. Maybe if she got a little closer.

Slipping out of her car, she crossed the parking lot and headed up the concrete walkway. Carefully staying out of the man's direct line of vision, she moved as close as she could. Drat! She still had no idea who he was.

The doors opened and closed again as the crew came back for another tree. As the workmen passed her, one leaned her way and warned, "If you're supposed to be working, honey, you'd better get busy. The big guys are on their way out."

The big guys? The motorcycle millionaires? Callie caught her bottom lip between her teeth.

The doors slid open with a muted whoosh.

Time stood still as Callie took in the tableau before her. Three men stood in the doorway, the one in the middle slightly ahead of the other two. They weren't wearing leather, but Callie knew these were the three founders of the company.

All the erotic details of her dreams swept through her mind. She looked at the two men in the back. The one on the left was blond. The other had dark brown hair. Both were tall, well built and undeniably handsome. The choice to wear helmets in the ad had obviously not been for aesthetic reasons.

A tendril of fear slithered up her back. There was one man left. She feared he wouldn't live up to her fantasies—she feared that he would. Guilt tugged at her conscience. How could she be feeling this way about another man, when she had so recently been in bed with Rorke?

She almost turned away, but couldn't resist the temptation. After all, she was only going to look. She would be crazy to pass up this opportunity.

As the men stepped outside, Callie looked at the one in the middle.

His head was turned to the side as he spoke to the man on his right.

Heavens, he was gorgeous.

He turned toward her and her breath caught in her throat. She felt the blood drain from her face. Her eyes must be playing strange tricks on her—he looked like Rorke.

His eyes met hers.

When she saw the flash of recognition in his, she knew. This man did not look like Rorke. He *was* Rorke.

Her vision blurred, and for a moment she thought she might faint, but then a warm familiar hand was clutching her arm.

"Callie, sweetheart, are you all right?"

The scene came partially back into focus. "I think so."

"What are you doing here?"

She looked up at him, not really seeing him. "I...I was waiting for you. I thought you came out here to apply for a job." That still could be the explanation. The other two might be the "big guys" and Rorke's vast experience had brought him to their attention and they'd interviewed him personally. Yes, of course, that must be it. But as her vision focused and she clearly saw the look on Rorke's face, Callie knew she was just grasping at straws. "You don't need an application, do you?"

He shook his head.

Someone laughed. "Damn, O'Neil, I know there's a good story here. But I've got a feeling it will be a long time before we hear it."

Callie looked behind Rorke and saw the two men smiling and watching her. She looked back to Rorke.

All the workmen were also watching. She straightened her shoulders, gathered up her control and refused to fall apart in front of an audience.

Rorke loosened his grip on her arm, moving his hand down to caress her elbow. "Since you're here, would you like to join us for lunch?"

She tried to mesh the images of her first love, the motorcycle millionaire and the fantasy white knight in leather with the man she'd made love with last night. Something inside her snapped. "Lunch?" She started to laugh. As she took two steps away from Rorke, Callie was able to see the man she'd gotten out of her car to observe.

Suddenly she remembered where she'd seen him before. He wasn't a resident of Harrison at all. He was the man with the briefcase who'd been at the garage and in Exeter arguing with Rorke. Oh, he must have laughed himself silly when she'd offered him money or a lawyer. She felt like an absolute fool!

"Callie?"

She looked around at all the spectators again before turning her angry gaze on Rorke. As soon as her eyes met his, everything flew from her mind except the knowledge that he'd lied to her. "Don't insult me by repeating your invitation."

He took a step forward, his palms facing up as he reached out for her. "Sweetheart—"

She stepped away, fighting back tears. "Don't touch me." He stopped and she continued. "How could you? After all that talk about trust." All the guilt she'd suffered on his behalf, all the hours she'd spent trying to puzzle out how to make him trust her again. Last night, he'd said he couldn't trust her because he didn't know her, all the time keeping this secret.

"Callie, why don't we go someplace where we can discuss this privately?"

Like a drenching with cold water, his words woke her up to the presence of their audience. She wanted to crawl into the newly planted bushes and disappear from sight.

Grandmother Harrison would be horrified if she knew what a spectacle Callie'd been making of herself. She'd never lost control of her temper in public before. She took a deep breath, counted to five and managed a cool smile.

"That won't be necessary, Mr. O'Neil. I wouldn't want to interfere with your plans." She turned and started to her car.

"Matt." Callie heard Rorke say as she forced herself to walk slowly.

"Yes, sir."

"Take Jesse and Alex to lunch. I'll meet you back here at one-thirty."

"Yes, sir."

Callie wasn't surprised when Rorke appeared at her side. When they reached her car, he opened the passenger door. She looked up at him, making no attempt to hide her fury. He looked back, challenging her to lose control again, daring her to make another scene.

Nine

Callie tilted her chin up, continuing to hold Rorke's gaze as she climbed gracefully into the passenger seat of her own car. Once he was in the driver's seat, she handed him the keys.

He started the car and headed out of the parking lot. The urge to explode at him faded and a soothing numbness settled over her like a wool cape. She sat by his side, silent, refusing to consider any of the questions she had and ignoring Rorke's attempts to talk to her.

He finally gave up and drove in silence back toward Harrison. When he reached the driveway leading to the town's newest home, he turned.

Callie remembered the last time she'd made the drive in darkness. *Don't think about it. Don't think about him ... don't think about us.* She curled more tightly into the calming numbness.

At the top of the driveway Rorke parked the car, got out and walked around to open her door. In a daze, she took the hand he offered to help her out, but released it once she was standing by his side.

She still felt detached and numb. With a hand set on her lower back, he guided her up the front steps. After opening the door, he stood back to let her enter. She walked in, glanced around the entry hall, then continued into the living room.

As she stepped onto the plush carpet, it was like stepping onto a cloud. The house had obviously been decorated by a professional. It was beautiful, elegant and worthy of a wealthy executive.

She walked to the front windows and stood looking out. ''No wonder his hands are softer,'' she said to herself.

Slowly she walked from room to room, only vaguely aware of Rorke following her. The numbness was slipping away and her mind was sifting through the past two weeks, picking up signs—small coincidences and inconsistencies she'd let slip past her at the time. Not just the fact his hands had less calluses, but his knowledge about Yankee and his custom bike, the sudden ordering of the skylight over the master bathtub—there was nothing supernatural about it and the site was not being bugged—Rorke had been standing right there when she'd jokingly mentioned it, and of course there was the man with the briefcase.

When her wandering brought her back to the entryway, Rorke asked if she'd like to see the upstairs.

"Upstairs?" She repeated the word several times. The fog she'd been walking in cleared. Turning to Rorke, her eyes lit with angry sparks.

He'd lied, not just to her, but to Steve and Rachel. Every time the plant was mentioned, every time the future owner of the house was mentioned, the evening they'd discussed the Yankee ad—every time he'd sat there and listened to them talk about the motorcycle millionaire, he'd been lying. Why? Why had he let them go on and on?

"No, I don't want to see the upstairs. I want some answers and then I want my car keys."

"One thing at a time, sweetheart. I'll give you your answers, but once I do, I don't think you'll be needing your keys."

"Don't bet on it." She turned and walked into the living room, then quickly turned again and headed back toward the door. She didn't need to hear the words from him. She knew why he'd lied. "On second thought, just give me the keys. I know why you did it. You wanted revenge, you wanted to hurt me the way I'd hurt you. Well, congratulations, you've succeeded."

He started to reach for her, but stopped when she took a step back. "Callie, let's sit down and talk."

She ignored his request. "I guess we're even now."

"Sweetheart, this wasn't about getting even. Let's go into the living room—"

A jolt of anger ran through her, leaving her hands quivering. Her inability to return to calmness, increased her ire. "No, this *was* about getting even. That's why you never answered my question about where we went from here. You had no intentions of trying to see if we could have a future together. I apologized, but that wasn't enough—you had to get even.'' She took a deep breath, trying to fight the tightening in her chest. ''But there's a big difference. I never meant to hurt you, I didn't plan it out or do it on purpose. I was young. I made the choice I did to protect you from my father. But you deliberately—''

He moved quickly, so quickly that he had hold of her shoulders before she had time to move beyond his grasp. ''That's enough, Callie. I know you're hurt and angry, but don't go making accusations until you've calmed down and heard my side of the story.''

''I see your side of the story. You left Harrison with nothing but a bad reputation, and came back a millionaire to rub our faces in it.''

''That's not how it is.''

''Isn't it? Open your eyes and look around. You picked a site level with and across from Harrison Manor. Look at the size and elegance of this house, Rorke.'' She moved back, out of his grasp, and raised her arms to the vaulted ceiling above. ''The day Steve showed us the house, you quite accurately said that now there was more than one castle in the kingdom.''

Rorke shrugged. ''I said that to annoy you. I picked this area for the house because it's near the plant and it holds special memories for me. Not to show off.''

She laughed in disbelief. ''You were showing off. Why else would you have come back to Harrison?''

''I know I was never a big favorite here, but it's still my hometown and I've missed it over the last ten years. When we started looking for new plant sites, I brought Alex and Jesse to Harrison. We bought the land and then once the project got underway, I decided to move up and run it.''

''And show off your new success to the town that shunned you.''

''I could have done that without moving back.''

''But this way, with you here in your castle, there's a constant reminder. Plus, by providing jobs for the area, jobs that will keep future generations from having to move away to make a living, you'll be in a real power position.''

''Callie, you know me well enough to know that I do things for my convenience and comfort, not to put on a display or to gain power over other people.''

She shook her head. ''No, no I don't know you at all. You're not my Rorke. You're a stranger. I don't know you. You've changed.''

''Of course I've changed. It's been ten years—surely you didn't expect me to be the same. Time changes people. Events change people. Heartbreak changes people. You walked out on me, it changed me. Nothing can undo that. Yes, I'm different than I was ten years ago, but so are you. We're both different people than we would have been if we'd gotten married. But we can't go back. There's no way to go back. Besides, you know me as well as you did last night when we were in bed together.''

He looked like the man she'd been with last night, but she didn't feel the same affinity for him that she'd felt then. ''Last night I went to bed with a man who doesn't exist.''

''I exist. I'm right here. I'm the man you were with last night.''

"No, I spent the night with an older version of a man I'd been in love with years ago. A mechanic—not a high-powered executive—just a mechanic."

"Some days that's exactly what I am."

"But that's not all you do."

"No, not anymore. Regardless, all that's changed since last night is that now you know I've got more money than you thought I did. Shouldn't that add to my score?"

"Not when the reason I didn't know was because you've been lying to me." A dull ache was beginning to build up behind her temples. "When were you going to tell me . . . or weren't you?"

"I was going to tell you this morning."

"Before or after we made love?"

"Instead of."

"I've heard enough." She started to walk past him but was stopped when he reached his arm out in front of her.

With his other hand he tilted her chin up until she was looking him in the eye. "Callie, I never lied to you."

"No? You call pretending to work for your father not lying?"

"I *am* working for my father. He lost one of his mechanics and hasn't been able to find a replacement."

"But you're not only working for your father."

"No, I'm not, but I never told you I was."

"It was still a lie of omission."

"It wasn't any of your business."

"Even after you asked me to spend the night with you last night? After you put me through hell because you said you could never trust me again?"

"All right, maybe it was your business and I've been meaning to tell you..."

A queasy feeling shifted through her. He'd obviously been keeping his identity a secret around Harrison—although how he was going to continue to do so once he moved into the house and the plant was operational, she had no idea. Maybe he didn't trust her to keep his secret.

She swallowed the lump forming in her throat. "You didn't trust me with the information, did you? You didn't think I would keep your secret."

"That has nothing to do with it. It was never a closely guarded secret. If anyone had done any extensive research on Yankee Motorworks, it would have been common knowledge by now. I only had the house built through the company so Steve wouldn't give me a discount."

Callie fought back the urge to rant and rave about the unfairness of it all. The temptation was strong to let loose and scream her frustrations. Let off some steam like she had earlier.

Suddenly, the specifics of Rorke's deception, the reasons, weren't important anymore. Even more important than the fact that he had been less than honest and up-front, and had betrayed the trust she'd placed in him...was the frightening way she'd acted when she'd confronted him at the Yankee plant. She'd forgotten where they were, who was there. She had acted like a complete stranger to herself.

Well, it wouldn't happen again, she vowed. And there was one way to ensure that it didn't. "It really doesn't matter, Rorke. In the long run, it just doesn't matter."

Fear crept into his eyes. His voice was little more than a whisper. "Callie?"

"I'd like my keys now."

"It's not over, Callie."

"I need time and space to think." Her words left the future open, but her eyes were saying her goodbyes.

He pulled the keys out of his pocket and looked down at them. "I should carry you upstairs and make love to you until you can't think anymore, until there is no time and space... just you and me."

He could do it; she knew he could. Desire flared up in her. Lord, she was tempted, tempted to make love with him one more time. But would she be able to walk away from him the day after tomorrow if she did?

For her own sanity, she had to walk away.

She held out her hand. He looked down at her and seemed about to say something. Instead he set the keys in her palm and walked past her into the living room.

Callie watched him over her shoulder, memorizing every movement, storing it away for the long years ahead. After he passed through the doorway leading to the dining room and kitchen, she headed out the front door.

Reaching her car, she stood and looked across the valley to Harrison Manor. The urge to go home swept over her.

Rorke came back into the living room after he heard the front door open and close. He stood looking out the window at Callie. She was facing away from him and hadn't gotten into her car yet. Did that mean she was thinking about coming back in?

God, he hoped so!

He was confident once she'd had time to calm down and think about it, everything would be all right. She'd been thrown off balance because of the way she'd found out about Yankee, but she'd come around.

He was glad she'd given herself to him before she knew the truth. It was proof that she wanted him and not his money.

As he watched, she opened the car door, got in and drove away without looking back. A knot tightened in the pit of his stomach. At the moment she didn't seem to want him *or* his money.

"You'll be seeing her this evening at the rehearsal," he reminded himself. She won't be running away this time. No matter how angry she was with him, he knew she wouldn't leave Rachel in the lurch.

Callie stood in the doorway of what had once been her room. It looked exactly as it had the night she'd left, and was obviously cleaned on a regular basis. The wood furniture was dust-free as were the glass doors in front of her Madame Alexander dolls. She walked over to her desk. Her high school yearbook sat in the middle, right where she'd left it. To the right was an assortment of pens and pencils in a holder she'd made in art one year—she didn't remember when.

She walked over to the window. Pushing aside several stuffed animals and a half-dozen ruffled throw pillows, she sat down on the window seat.

Ten years ago, she'd sat in this same spot and made the decision that had changed her life...and Rorke's.

She looked out the window toward town and O'Neil's garage. Looking at what had once been Rorke's bedroom window. The window she herself had looked out little more than twelve hours ago—it seemed like a lifetime.

She shifted her gaze to look at Rorke's new house. It hurt too much to think about him. She got up and went over to the bed.

Nan, her father's housekeeper, had told her that her father would be home at two o'clock for lunch. That gave her a little over an hour before she had to leave.

Laying down, she closed her eyes. "Just for a few minutes," she told herself. "Just until the headache goes away."

"Callie?"

The sound of someone calling her name pulled her from a disturbing dream of a knight in black armor jousting with a knight in silver so bright, it shone white.

"Callie, honey."

She opened her eyes. Her father's housekeeper stood next to the bed looking down at her. "Nan, I'm sorry. I guess I fell asleep."

"That's all right. You look like you could use the rest, but I thought you might want to know your father is here."

Callie looked at her watch. Two o'clock. Darn! Why had she slept so long? "Did you tell him I'm here?"

"Only because he asked whose car was in the driveway."

"What did he say?"

"Just asked for lunch to be served on the patio and told me to be sure to set the table for two."

Callie ran her hands through her hair. "I need to freshen up a bit."

Nan set her hand on Callie's shoulder. "I'm glad you came, Callie. Your father is stubborn and I don't think he would ever have made the first move, but I know he's glad you're here."

Callie got off the bed and headed toward the bathroom. "I'll be down in a minute."

She was beginning to regret her impulsive visit. After the wrenching emotions of learning the truth about Rorke, did she really want to add a confrontation with her father?

The peace and security of a familiar place was what she'd run home for. She didn't want to see her father. She shouldn't have come. But there was no backing out now.

Once she looked as presentable as possible, considering the distress she'd been in, she went downstairs to the patio.

Chandler Harrison stood as his daughter walked toward him. He'd aged considerably in the past ten years. "I had heard you were in town."

"I came for Rachel's wedding."

Nan came bustling out. "Shall I serve lunch now, Mr. Harrison?"

"Please." After the housekeeper left, he motioned to the chair across from him. "Have a seat, Calista."

He hadn't ordered her off the premises. That was a good sign. Callie sat down, picked up her napkin and placed it in her lap.

Her father took his seat. "You look well. How have you been?"

"Fine. And you?"

"I'm sure your grandmother has kept you adequately informed about me."

"Actually, she has." Although she hadn't mentioned how much he'd aged.

"I had assumed as much. She keeps me equally informed about you."

"Did she preface her reports by saying, 'Not that you're interested, but...'?"

"Yes, and she always ends by telling me what a stubborn fool I am."

Callie smiled. "She called me an ungrateful whippersnapper."

Chandler laughed and relaxed more in his chair.

Nan arrived with lunch. Once they were alone again, her father began telling Callie anecdotes about the morning's customers. It was the same type of conversation they'd had over many a meal when she'd lived here. Neither mentioned the fact that the last time they'd lunched together had been ten years before.

Over coffee and dessert, Callie told him about the upcoming wedding.

"I hear Rorke O'Neil is going to be the best man."

From the narrowing of his eyes and the pulling together of his eyebrows, Callie suspected that wasn't all he'd heard. He probably knew they'd been out to dinner together and might even know she'd been with him overnight.

Was he going to reissue his threats against her being with Rorke? It wouldn't make a difference in her current relationship with Rorke, but it would ruin the tentative ties she and her father were forming. "Yes, he's going to be the best man."

Chandler nodded, but didn't say anything more.

Nan came out to collect the empty plates. "More coffee?"

Chandler looked at his watch. "I've got to get back to work. If it was any day but Friday, I'd take the rest of the afternoon off." He stood up and came around to Callie's side of the table.

Callie also stood. "I understand."

"When are you going back?"

"I plan to leave on Sunday."

"Any chance you could come by again before you go?"

After the wedding, Rachel and Steve would be heading off for the honeymoon, leaving her alone at Rachel's house for the night. She hadn't minded the thought of staying alone before, but she wondered if she might be safer from Rorke at Harrison Manor— not that she was afraid of him doing anything. What worried her was that she might give in to the temptation of spending one last night in his arms. "I could come by after the wedding, spend the night and leave from here Sunday. If it's all right with you."

"That sounds fine." Her father's eyes looked watery as he reached out and hugged her to him. "Well, whippersnapper, you do know this stubborn fool missed you."

Callie nodded her yes, not trusting herself to speak. "I'll see you on Saturday, then."

After her father left, Callie went to the kitchen to tell Nan she would be coming back tomorrow night. Nan walked out to the front of the house with her. Callie carefully avoided looking across the valley to Rorke's.

After saying goodbye, she headed to Rachel's, hoping she wouldn't find Rorke waiting for her when she got there.

Ten

Rorke hadn't been at Rachel's and hadn't shown up over the course of the afternoon, although Callie's ears had been tuned for the sound of his arrival.

Now it was time for them to leave for the rehearsal and she knew he would be there.

"Why don't you let me drive? Then you can have Rorke bring you home from the rehearsal dinner. Just be sure he gets you back in time for breakfast," Rachel teased, closing the door between the kitchen and the garage.

All afternoon she'd wanted to tell Rachel about Rorke and Yankee, but if she told Rachel, then Rachel would tell Steve, and probably her mother, and the news would spread like wildfire, completely eclipsing the wedding. "No, I'll drive. I'm going to make sure you get home in plenty of time to get your beauty rest and make sure you and Steve stay away from each other after midnight. It's bad luck for the groom to see the bride before the wedding on their wedding day.''

Rachel raised one brow. "How does Rorke feel about your plans?"

"It's none of his business." Callie walked down the driveway to her car. She heard the garage door closing, then Rachel's footsteps behind her.

"Hey, did I miss something? You don't sound anything like the woman who floated through my door this morning."

"I wasn't completely awake. Once I fully woke up, I realized I'd made a mistake last night." Rachel looked stunned. "Listen, today and tomorrow are *your* days. Let's focus on that."

"But this morning—"

Callie got into her car. Rachel joined her. Callie had risked facing Rorke to ask for a truce so their past relationship wouldn't affect the wedding. They'd formed a truce and then some, and now their present relationship was jeopardizing the serenity of the events ahead.

She sighed. "Rach, last night was incredible, but there's more to a relationship than great sex. Rorke and me . . . there's no way it would work out."

"Does he know yet?"

"Yes. I . . . I saw him before I went up to Harrison Manor." She started the car and pulled away from the curb.

"Did he agree with you?" Rachel asked.

"Not exactly."

"Then there's still hope."

Callie glanced over at her friend. Rachel wore a smug smile. If she knew the full story, she would know how hopeless the situation was, but this was supposed to be a happy time, so Callie changed the subject for the remainder of the drive to the church.

There was no sign of either of Rorke's motorcycles in the parking lot when Callie pulled in and parked. And still no sign of him by the time the other members of the wedding party were assembled at the front of the church.

While they were waiting, Callie slipped away from Rachel and the other bridesmaids to where Steve was talking with several of his ushers. She gave him the ring she hadn't remembered to give Rorke earlier in the day.

"By the way, what's keeping Rorke?" Steve asked.

Rachel must have told Steve about last night. Either that, or Rachel's neighbors had already spread the word. What on earth had she been thinking of this morning? "I have no idea."

"He's probably catching up on his sleep," Rachel's brother said.

The group laughed. Callie felt the blood rush to her cheeks. Obviously, news of her night with Rorke had been making the rounds. Terrific. Just what she needed.

She went back to the bride's side of the church. As the minutes ticked by, Callie's imagination began coming up with reasons for Rorke's absence: a flat tire, an empty gas tank, an accident, a boycott of the rehearsal because he knew she would be there, a broken heart. . . .

The double doors at the rear of the church swung open and he was there.

"Sorry I'm late." He was all right. Callie was so relieved to see him safe, she had a hard time keeping herself from running to him.

When he reached the front of the church, the ring-bearer looked up at him and blurted out, "You don't look like a jumbo, tattooed biker dude to me! My mom said—"

"Jeremy!" Jeremy's mother jumped up and put her hand over her son's mouth. She shrugged and smiled weakly at Rorke as she led the boy over to the front pew where she'd been sitting.

"Shall we begin, then?" the minister asked.

The rehearsal went smoothly. Callie deliberately didn't look in Rorke's direction, although she could feel his gaze on her.

As the minister began describing the recessional, Rachel's cousin from Michigan bumped Callie with her elbow. "I'd trade partners with you in a heartbeat. The best man's a real dreamboat."

Callie managed a weak smile in return. She wished they could trade, too. Walking down the aisle on Rorke's arm would be the hardest part of the ceremony for her.

When it was their turn, he held out his elbow. She moved her arm behind his and placed her hand on his forearm. He pulled his arm in closer to his body and her breath caught as a jolt of awareness shot through her. She quickened her steps, trying to reach the end of the aisle.

"Miss Harrison, this is a recessional, not a race," the minister called out over the sound of the church organ. She felt the blood rush to her cheeks.

Callie heard Rachel's brother say something but couldn't hear what it was. She knew she wouldn't have liked it though by the way his partner giggled.

When they reached the back of the church, Rorke kept hold of her arm while the minister gave them his final instructions. Several times she tried to pull away, but he gently tightened his hold.

She looked up at him. He looked back.

"Angry that I was late?" he whispered.

"Were you late?"

He grinned mischievously. "Didn't you miss me?"

"Not likely."

Callie turned her attention back to the business at hand.

"If there are no further questions, I think we can adjourn," the minister said.

Rachel had arranged for a combination rehearsal dinner and decorating party to be held in the parish center.

Callie started to step toward the door, but Rorke held her back. "We need to talk."

She bit her tongue and waited until they were alone. Before the door had completely closed behind the last person, she pulled free of him. "We have nothing to talk about."

"We have everything to talk about." He stuck his hands in his rear pockets. "I gave you time and space."

"One afternoon . . . You gave me one afternoon."

"How much time do you want, Callie? Ten years?"

A knot formed in the pit of her stomach. She took a deep breath and let it out slowly. "This isn't the time or the place. If we don't show up at the parish center soon, someone will notice we're both missing, and we agreed that we wouldn't let our problems get in the way of Rachel's wedding."

"These are not the same issues we came to an agreement on."

"Granted, but I still think we should get on with our roles in the wedding party and keep our personal affairs out of the picture."

"Hey, you're the one who's kept her nose in the air, refusing to even acknowledge my presence. That kind of behavior will draw just as much attention as if we were arguing openly."

"I'm trying not to feed the rumor mill."

He laughed. "That didn't seem to bother you this morning when you nearly seduced me in Rachel's driveway."

"I nearly seduced you? Is that what everyone is saying?" How on earth was she going to face them tomorrow? Darn, how had she gotten into this mess?

"No, that's my interpretation of the morning. The story on the grapevine is that we were at each other all night long and then almost did it one last time in the middle of Maple Street."

Callie sighed as she closed her eyes and shook her head. "I don't believe this."

"I warned you we were being watched this morning, but you said you didn't care."

She opened her eyes. "It didn't matter this morning. Not when I thought that I...that we..." She had thought they had a future together, that last night had been just the beginning. Running her hands through her hair in frustration, she continued. "I thought any rumors about the two of us being an item would be true."

He folded his arms across his chest, the last remnants of his smile faded. "You don't consider us an item?"

Looking down at his shoes, she shook her head. She'd known he wouldn't be happy with her decision and had wanted to avoid the subject until after the wedding, but he didn't leave her much choice. "Not anymore."

"One little bump in the road and you're going to bail out?"

She looked up at him. If she told him her fears for her sanity and her self-control, she knew he would try to soothe her and reassure her. As vulnerable as she was to him, she knew she'd fall right into his arms. So instead, she chose to focus on his neglecting to tell her about Yankee Motorworks. "Little bump! By your standards maybe—not by mine. I think honesty is a very important issue."

Closing the space between them, he threaded his hands through her hair. His touch was gentle, but his gaze was hard. "From where I'm sitting it doesn't look like you've been completely honest with me, either."

"When have I lied to you?"

"When you told me you weren't a one-night stand."

Without waiting for her to respond, he turned around and walked out of the church. Callie stared after him in disbelief. Slowly she counted to ten, fighting back the urge to send a hymnal flying after him.

A one-night stand!

He was accusing her of being a one-night stand. She'd wanted so much more from him—a lifetime of nights... and days. But nights and days when she still had command over her own behavior and emotions.

Once she was calmer, she made her way over to the parish center. The group was in a lively, festive mood. The ladies were still laying out the food on the buffet table for the rehearsal dinner, and the men, under Rachel's direction, were hanging crepe paper, blowing up balloons and setting up tables and chairs for tomorrow. Rorke was busy helping with the chairs.

Callie walked into the kitchen to lend a hand.

Rachel spotted her right away, came up and swiped her finger through the frosting on the cake Callie was slicing. "I was beginning to think I'd have to send out a search party."

"I was hoping no one would notice."

"Just me." Rachel patted her on the shoulder. "Everything all right?"

She managed a smile. "Everything's just fine."

"Rorke didn't look fine when he walked in here. And while you look cool as a cucumber, I think things are far from fine."

"Rachel, believe me, I'm fine."

Rachel threw her hands up in resignation. "All right, if you say so."

"I say so." Callie picked up the cake and carried it out to the dessert table.

Over the next few hours, the group ate and worked on fixing the spacious room for the next day's reception. By the time they were finished, all that remained was for the florist to deliver the flowers and the caterer to arrive with the food and champagne.

Callie managed to stay away from Rorke. She suspected this was made easier by his efforts as well as her own. Rachel's cousin seemed to be set on doing the opposite. Every time Callie spotted Rorke across the room, the petite redhead was in his immediate area.

So, what's it to you? The sooner he takes up with someone else the sooner he'll leave you alone.

She believed her own advice, but that didn't stop the sharp stab of pain she felt imagining Rorke and Rachel's cousin in an intimate embrace. Even overhearing two of the ushers comment that the woman from the bachelor party was happily married, didn't raise her spirits. Yesterday the same information would have thrilled her.

As the group left the building, a cheer rose up from the people gathered in the park across the street.

Rachel looked up at Steve. "What on earth . . . ?"

"Don't look at me."

All the streetlights went off and a shrill whistling sounded moments before the first of the colorful fireworks burst and lit the sky. An assortment of oohs and aahs rose from the crowd.

Everyone was looking at the sky except Callie. She was watching Rorke. She could see the flashes of light reflected in his eyes.

From the sounds coming from the crowd it appeared there had been a good turnout. In the dark she felt protected, but tomorrow she would have to face them knowing most of them knew she'd spent last night with Rorke. Ultimately, she didn't care what the town thought. Thinking about them was only a futile attempt to stop thinking about Rorke and what might have been.

She had been watching him for quite a while before she realized he was no longer looking up, but straight at her. She turned away. Usually she loved fireworks, but tonight she wanted the show to end quickly. It had been a long day—she was ready for it to be over.

The finale lit the sky to cheers and clapping. The lights came back on.

Rachel turned to Callie. "You did this, didn't you?"

"I had a lot of help getting it arranged."

"But it was your idea, right?"

"Yes."

Rachel hugged her. "Thank you. The fireworks were wonderful."

Steve spoke up, "Just wait until you see the fireworks I have in store for you tomorrow night."

A chorus of catcalls and whistles broke out among the high-spirited ushers. Rachel tried to look stern, but ended up laughing.

Callie couldn't stop herself from looking in Rorke's direction and remembering the fireworks that had exploded between them. He was looking back at her, and from the heat in his eyes, she knew he was thinking about the same thing.

A deep yearning ache began building inside her. An ache she knew only Rorke would ever be able to satisfy completely. *Get over it, Callie. There's no future there.*

Rorke watched Callie head toward the parking lot. He'd expected her to have gotten over her anger at him. Obviously, she hadn't. And he was having serious doubts that she ever would.

So what? Who needed her?

There were plenty of other women in the world... the charming little redhead for one. She'd been sending him come-hither looks all evening.

If Alex and Jesse wouldn't have been staying at the house, he might have considered taking her home with him. *Sure, pal, and if you keep telling yourself that all the way home, you might just begin to believe it.*

Callie woke during the night, her pulse racing. She couldn't remember her dream, but the physical effects it had on her were disturbing, leading her to suspect she'd been dreaming of Rorke.

Why was her body doing this to her—letting Rorke invade her dreams, and when she woke, letting her nerve endings be alive with the memory of his touch?

She got up and washed her face with cool water. As she headed back to her room, she noticed the light was on in the kitchen.

She entered the room and found Rachel at the table with a box of tissues on her left and a small crumpled stack of them on her right.

Callie sat down across from her friend. ''Rachel, what's wrong?''

Rachel sniffled and wiped at her eyes. ''Everything is ready for the wedding, and before you know it, Steve and I will be married.''

''Are these tears of joy, then? You don't look very happy.''

''I should be, shouldn't I? But this is my last night here in the house Carl and I lived in and...and I started thinking about him and about our wedding, the day we closed on this house, the day we hung this wallpaper..."

Callie reached out and took her hand, squeezing gently. "Rachel..." she began, then stopped. *What could she say?*

Rachel had married her high school sweetheart. They'd been happy together, until three years ago when Carl had been killed. He'd been an excellent skier, and frequently was called on for search-and-rescue detail—he hadn't returned from his last trip.

"I love Steve so much, I really do, but I still love Carl, too."

"I'm sure Steve understands there will always be a part of you that loves Carl. And I'm just as sure Carl would be glad you have Steve. I know he wouldn't want you to spend the rest of your life alone."

Alone, the word echoed through her mind. No, no one should have to face being alone indefinitely. While she did believe it, she also knew she would be alone in the years to come. No man would ever replace Rorke in her heart.

"It was a Ferrari. I know it was. Didn't you see the logo?"

Callie looked up as Rachel's aunt and cousin exploded into the bridal room at the church. Between them they carried a bridesmaid dress, shoes dyed to match, a makeup case, electric curlers, a blow-dryer and a copy of *Cosmopolitan.*

"Hi, all. You'll never guess what we saw this morning." Rachel's cousin plunked herself down in the final vacant chair.

"What we *might* have seen," her mother corrected.

The two of them started unpacking their supplies. "It was a Ferrari. Can you believe it?"

Callie could. She'd seen it yesterday at the Yankee plant. She assumed it belonged to one of the other two owners. Apparently they were still in town. She wondered if Rorke would be bringing them to the wedding.

Localized conversations started up again around the room as the women prepared for the event ahead.

Rachel looked at Callie. "The house is finished. Maybe Harrison's newest citizen has arrived."

"Maybe." Callie applied a subtle streak of blush to each cheek. "By any chance, did Rorke say anything about bringing any guests?"

"Actually he did. Last night he told Steve he had a few friends visiting from New York and asked if he could bring them along. Anyone you know?"

"Not really, but I may have seen them yesterday."

"Male?"

"Oh, yes."

There was a knock at the door. The photographer had arrived.

The next hour flew by and before she knew it, Callie found herself standing in the open doorway leading into St. Paul's.

Eleven

Callie was careful to avoid looking directly at the end of the aisle. As she stepped onto the white runner, she watched the back of the bridesmaid in front of her, refusing to let her eyes shift to the right. But as she reached her place to the left of the minister and turned to face the rear of the church for the entrance of the bride, she allowed herself one short peek at Rorke.

Her heart picked up its pace as she saw he looked as gorgeous in his gray tuxedo as she'd imagined he would.

She forced her attention to the sight of Rachel coming toward them on her father's arm. One look at the smile on the bride's face and it was clear how much she loved her soon-to-be husband and how confident she felt in her decision to marry him, all signs of last night's uneasiness gone. Rachel's father placed her hand into Steve's and the ceremony began.

"Dearly beloved, we are gathered here to join together this man and this woman in holy matrimony."

The familiar words of the wedding vows faded into the background and became like the sound of waves lapping gently at the edges of Callie's conscious mind. She couldn't help thinking about the wedding that should have been ten years ago.

It wouldn't have been on this scale. No flower-bedecked church, no attendants in matching attire, no pews full of friends and family, but the vows would have been the same. The same bonding together of two hearts . . . two lives.

She fought back tears, knowing it wouldn't be the only time she'd have to do it today. Of course it wasn't crucial for her to stay dry-eyed—lots of people cried at weddings. Granted, the other tears would be tears of happiness. But no one would know the difference.

She *was* glad for her friend. Rachel deserved happiness. As the ceremony continued, Callie's attention refocused on the couple promising themselves to each other today, and the tears that finally rolled down her cheeks were tears of joy.

When it came time for the exchange of rings, she thought back to yesterday. If she'd only kept the other ring until last night . . . so much might be different.

She'd probably still be in the dark, thinking Rorke was working for his father. *Maybe*. Or maybe Rorke *would* have told her about Yankee by now. If she'd heard it from him, rather than discovering it on her own, what would she have done?

Over the heads of the kneeling couple, her eyes met Rorke's. The two bouquets she held made a rustling noise as they bumped together in her shaky hands. She wanted to look away, but couldn't. It was an opportunity to memorize every detail of him without being caught in an argument or other unpleasant conversation.

The look on his face was unreadable. No softness or tenderness, no love or desire in his eyes—his expression was cool, almost arrogant.

The bride and groom stood. Callie handed Rachel her bridal bouquet and returned her attention to the ceremony. After a few final words, the minister introduced the newly married couple to the gathered guests. There was a flurry of applause and the recessional music began.

She was glad they'd practiced this the night before, so she wasn't caught off guard by the jolt of awareness that came when she tucked her arm around Rorke's. She still felt it, but it didn't surprise her and she was able to mask her reaction from the many eyes watching them.

As they walked side by side down the aisle, Callie saw Rorke's partners. The blonde winked at her as she passed. Rorke must have seen the exchange; he seemed to be fighting back a smile. No doubt he was remembering what a fool she'd made of herself yesterday.

She also noticed they were getting curious looks from the hometown guests—the people who had watched them grow up, the people who had watched their antics over the past few days.

Michael O'Neil was sitting toward the back of the church and flashed her a friendly smile. Rorke obviously hadn't confided their latest troubles to his father.

As they exited out the arched doorway, Rorke whispered, "Well, Ms. Harrison, you've walked down the aisle of St. Paul's on my disreputable arm, and the ghosts of your hallowed ancestors didn't rise up in protest nor bolts of lightning strike us dead."

There was no further chance for conversation as the photographer began choreographing the group pictures. Even with Rorke on the other side of the happy couple, Callie found herself being swept up in the joyous mood of the occasion.

Her happy mood lasted until Rorke stood up to make the traditional best man's toast to the newlyweds. There was a flurry of whispers when he first stood, but the authority in his voice as he asked for everyone's attention quickly brought quiet to the group. It was easy for Callie to picture him in the Yankee boardroom conducting a meeting.

"As Reverend Bartlett said earlier, a wedding is a celebration of love. But exchanging wedding vows is only part of the process needed to nurture the special gift of love between two people. It needs to be cherished, protected and fought for. Being in love may feel like heaven at times, however, both partners need to remember we are not celestial beings. We are human, and humans make mistakes. But when you love deeply enough, there's room for forgiveness and compromise. I wish you many years of heaven and peaceful compromises." He lifted his glass. "To Steve and Rachel."

An assortment of "Here, here," and "Cheers," echoed around the room. More than one person swiped away a tear or two. Callie did. For the love she'd lost and found, only to lose again.

The bandleader called the bride and groom to the dance floor. An uneasy feeling started in the pit of Callie's stomach. She'd forgotten about this part of the event. First the newlyweds would dance, next the parents would be called out and then the wedding party. The last thing she wanted was to be in Rorke's arms on the dance floor.

No—actually the last thing she wanted was to make a scene. So, reluctant or not, she knew when the time came she would go complacently.

When it was their turn, Rorke walked to where she was sitting and held out his hand. Keeping her eyes on his palm, she set her own on it. His strong fingers curled around hers. It was hard not to think about the pleasure she'd received from his hands and how shocked everyone would be if they knew half the places his hands had roamed and how much she'd loved every minute.

She stood and followed him to the dance floor. He took her into his arms.

Callie focused on the music—anything to keep her mind off the man holding her. A love song, of course. What else at a wedding?

A song about eternal love, love that lasted as long as the winds blew and the stars shone. Beautiful, poetic, the kind of love to think about on wedding days. Callie knew it existed. She'd been so close to it—close enough to feel its comfort—close enough to feel its heat.

She could feel it even now, her body aligned so intimately to his. She couldn't help thinking about the times they'd been locked in each other's arms without the layers of clothing that now separated them.

She could feel him watching her, silently urging her to look up. But she couldn't.

If she looked in his eyes, she would be lost.

His words about cherishing, protecting and fighting for true love, kept circling in her mind. She knew his message had been meant for her as well as the bridal couple. She realized it was the first time, since her return, that he'd verbally admitted he still loved her.

But what if love threatened your peace of mind, your ability to function normally and stay in control?

Shoving the unanswerable questions from her mind, she concentrated on dancing. They'd never danced together before.

He was a good dancer, leading her gently and expertly. For the first time, she felt like the golden-haired princess he'd accused her of being. He, of course, was the handsome prince. Automatically her head tilted back and her gaze moved up—oh, how he looked the part as he smiled.

The rest of the room faded away. All the reality that existed were the soft lights, the tantalizing lyrics and Rorke. It seemed perfectly natural for him to lean forward and place his mouth over hers. She let her eyelids drift closed.

Whistles and catcalls pulled her out of the lethargy she'd slipped into. She'd only danced with him so she wouldn't make a scene and then she turned around and made one anyway.

Why, why couldn't she turn the hands of the clock twenty-four hours ahead so all this would be over and she would be on her way home. *Be honest, Callie. You don't want to move the clock ahead, you want to move it back.* Back? As she thought about it, she realized she did want the clock to move back.... Forty-eight hours didn't seem much to ask. Forty-eight hours back to the night she'd been naked in his arms. Ignorant of his deception, completely unaware that her world was about to come crashing down around her.

She concentrated once again on the music, until Rorke's voice cut into her thoughts. "You're going to run away again, aren't you?"

Callie looked up at him, carefully schooling her features to show no emotions. "No. I'm going home. I came here for my best friend's wedding. It's over. She's married now and I'm leaving just as I'd planned to do when I arrived. Sticking to my original plans is not running away."

"Callie, don't do this to me...to us. We've been given a second chance. Don't throw it away."

Steve came up behind Rorke and tapped him on the shoulder. "Time for musical partners. Your turn with the bride, Rorke."

With one last heated look at Callie, Rorke turned to where Rachel was waiting.

Steve held his hand out to Callie. "Looks like all this love and wedding stuff may be contagious."

"I'm not sure I know what you mean."

"I was referring to Rorke's kissing you."

"Oh, that. Just the traditional kiss between the best man and the maid of honor."

Steve chuckled. "Must be a new tradition, because I've been best man in several weddings and have yet to kiss the maid of honor."

Rachel's father cut in next, followed by several of the ushers, Steve's father, a few of her cousins and her uncle. When she was finally able to get away, she found a spot in a quiet corner and sat down, hoping for a moment alone to collect herself.

Her plans for peace vanished as a small elderly woman wandered over and sat down next to her.

"That O'Neil boy sure cleans up nicely, doesn't he?"

You could always count on Miss Dunsworth—Callie's former teacher—to say the last thing you would expect from her. Callie fought back the urge to laugh. "Yes, ma'am."

"If I were thirty years younger..." She sighed, and patted the side of her head. "I had my hair done this morning."

"It looks very nice."

"Phooey." She waved off Callie's compliment. "It looks the same as it did yesterday and the day before, as well." Miss Dunsworth had worn her hair in the same style as far back as Callie could remember. Patting the other side of her hair, she continued. "I could do this myself, you know. But then I would miss the latest news. This morning's news was especially interesting."

"Really?"

"Don't be coy with me, Calista Harrison. You've been seeing that boy, haven't you?"

There was no doubt Rorke was the "boy" in question. "We were both in the wedding party."

Miss Dunsworth didn't contradict her, but gave her a look which any Harrison High graduate could identify. It was the look she gave students who claimed the dog had eaten their homework.

"Listen, dear, you don't have to make any excuses to me. I'm on your side, one hundred percent."

"My side?"

"Yes, your side. And let me tell you something. If you want him, have him and tell everyone else to go stuff it. And you can quote me on that."

Callie put her arms around Miss Dunsworth and hugged her. "I appreciate your support."

"So will there be another wedding soon? I just love weddings."

"No." Callie shook her head. She looked out to the dance floor where Rorke was dancing with Rachel's cousin, holding her close and smiling down at her. Silently she apologized for the lie she was about to tell the older woman, especially after she'd offered her support. "There's nothing between Rorke and me, other than our both being in the wedding."

"Hogwash." Miss Dunsworth dismissed Callie's claim. "Listen to me, young lady, don't let the prejudices and opinions of well-meaning friends and family force you into spending your life alone."

There was so much emotion in the woman's voice, Callie wondered if she was speaking from personal experience. She'd never heard Miss Dunsworth complain about being single. She'd always assumed it was by choice, since she'd never seemed dissatisfied or unhappy. Before Callie had a chance to reply, Rorke's friend, who had winked at her in church, came up and asked her to dance.

Miss Dunsworth spoke up. "Do I know you, young man? You look very familiar."

"I don't believe so." He reached out his right hand to her. "Alex Dalton. I work with Rorke O'Neil."

After looking closely at his hand, Miss Dunsworth shook it. "You've got clean fingers for a mechanic."

Alex looked puzzled, but didn't question her. He looked back to Callie. Before she could answer Miss Dunsworth answered for her, "Go ahead, dear. I'll talk to you later. In the meantime—" she pointed at Alex "—I'm going to try to remember where I've seen you before."

Miss Dunsworth's memory was legendary. Callie suspected Alex had been the Yankee owner who'd been featured in the local paper.

Once they were on the dance floor Alex asked, "Was that a relative or just a chaperone?"

"Neither, my high school algebra teacher. Actually, she was the algebra teacher for about half the people here. She has a tendency to mother her former students."

"If I remember correctly, your name is Callie, right?"

She nodded, embarrassed as she recalled that he'd heard her name yesterday from Rorke.

"Is it your given name or a nickname?"

"It's short for Calista. It was my great-grandmother's name. Is Alex short for Alexander?"

"Technically, but if you call me Alexander I probably won't answer."

"Alex, it is then."

He wasn't her type, but she could appreciate his masculine appeal. She wondered which of the men on the billboard he was. It came to her that she didn't even know which one Rorke was. She'd been attracted to the one in white, and Rorke had been standing in the middle yesterday as they'd walked out of the building, but that didn't mean he'd been in the middle in the photo. The white knight of her dreams could just as easily be the man she was dancing with now.

"So, tell me, Alex, in the Yankee ad, which one are you? Red, white or blue?"

Alex smiled. "How do you know I'm there at all?"

"Aren't you?"

"I suppose Rorke told you. I'm the one in blue."

She caught her bottom lip between her teeth. The odds were now fifty-fifty. Smiling up at him, she asked, "And which was Rorke?"

"Didn't he tell you?"

"Actually, I never asked."

He shrugged. "Just to be on the safe side, I'd better not say." His gaze dropped to her lips and then slid lower. With the hand resting on her back, he pulled her closer. "However, if you promise me another dance, I'll tell you which one is Jesse."

"All right."

"Jesse's in red."

That meant Rorke *was* the one in white, the one she'd been dreaming about. Had she recognized him on some deep level? Had the strange reaction she'd had to the billboard been a message from her subconscious?

She was so wrapped up in her thoughts, she almost missed the flicker of male interest in Alex's eyes. *Terrific, just what she needed.* Glancing to the side, she noticed Rorke watching her over the head of his dance partner.

A bolt of jealousy hit her. *Don't, Callie. You don't want him. So let him get on with his life and you get on with yours.* Defiantly, she smiled up at Alex.

"From your actions yesterday, and from bits and pieces I've overheard today, I take it not many people around here know Rorke is with Yankee."

"Maybe you should ask Rorke about this."

"I have. He's not talking."

"Then maybe I shouldn't, either."

"What about the details of your relationship with him? Will you discuss those?"

"No."

"Then how about answering one question for me?"

Callie shrugged. "That depends on what it is."

"Are you available or unavailable?"

As attractive as he was, he wasn't Rorke. And while she didn't want Rorke, or at least was trying to convince herself she didn't, she had to admit she didn't want anyone else either. "Unavailable."

The song came to an end. The bandleader announced they would be taking a break and the bride and groom would be throwing the garter to the eligible bachelors and the bouquet to the single women.

Alex left her to join in. After much teasing Steve tossed the garter toward the rowdy group of men. Standing near the middle of the crowd, Rorke jumped up and easily caught it. There were several appreciative female yells from the women gathering for the bouquet toss. Callie stood well away from the group, watching.

As the men dispersed, Alex walked back to her. "When you said you were unavailable, I didn't realize you meant you were married."

"I'm not married."

"Then why aren't you over there trying to catch the bouquet?"

"I don't want to catch it."

"Don't want to be the next bride?"

Callie shook her head. "No."

"Callie, get over here!" Rachel had spotted her.

She stood in the back of the pack, but the bouquet came right to her anyway. Callie smiled stiffly as she and Rorke posed with Rachel and Steve, the garter and the bouquet. Just when she thought she was home free, the photographer suggested he get a shot of Rorke putting the garter on her.

Someone brought out a chair and she sat down. Rorke went down on one knee in front of her. Luckily, the flowers she held masked the shaking of her hands.

The crowd was loving every minute of this, judging by the cheers and catcalls. *At least someone was having a good time.* Callie wished she could shrink down small enough to crawl into the bouquet.

The photographer arranged her dress so it was just above her knee, and he positioned Rorke's hands and the garter just below. Her heart was racing and twinges of arousal were escalating rapidly to an uncomfortable level—uncomfortable only because she and Rorke were in a public place and weren't free to take advantage of those feelings.

She was grateful when the photographer said he was finished. As she lowered her dress, Rorke moved his hands farther up, dragging the garter with them. Spreading his fingers, he reached up to skim the sensitive skin of her thigh. Callie sucked in her breath.

When he finally pulled his hands out from under her dress, they were empty. She could feel the garter hugging her leg.

Rorke stood and looked down at her. "If you'd like help getting that off, you know where to find me."

Twelve

Months of careful planning had paid off—the wedding and reception had been a huge success from the moment the first guest arrived at the church until the last handful of rice was thrown at the fleeing couple.

Callie swiped a tear off her cheek with one hand, waving goodbye with the other. As she lowered her arm, she realized she was holding a mauve ribbon rose from one of the rice bags. Her mind drifted back to the day she'd gone into Exeter to buy the ribbon. The day Rorke had almost kissed her. So much water had passed under the bridge since then.

As the crowd began dispersing, she returned to the bridal room to gather up her personal belongings. Arms full, she set off for her car.

When she stepped into the parking lot, Alex appeared at her elbow.

"Can I help you with some of that?"

"I've got it, but if you wouldn't mind opening my trunk." She jangled the key ring hanging on her finger.

Alex maneuvered around the things she held and managed to get her keys. He walked ahead of her and had the trunk open and ready when she got there. Callie put everything down except the bridal bouquet. Alex closed the lid.

Returning her keys, he closed his hand over hers. He looked down at her. The hint of interest she'd noticed earlier still evident.

"No wonder Rorke wants to move up here to the middle of nowhere."

"If you're implying I have anything to do with it, you're mistaken."

"I have to disagree. You're well worth the move."

"Thank you for the compliment, but since I live in New York..." She removed her hand from his and pointed to the license plate on the back of her car.

He smiled, a wide smile complete with dimple on his right cheek. "New York, huh?"

Before she could remind him of her earlier answer to his question of her availability, Rorke cut in. "Yes, she lives in New York, and I'll give you a little free advice." He put his arm around Alex's shoulder and leaned toward him, keeping his voice low so only Alex and Callie could hear. "Dust off your best sob story. She's a real sucker for a sob story. Throw in a little moonlight and the sky's the limit."

No one heard Rorke's remarks, but everyone milling around the parking lot heard Callie's response. "How dare you say those things about me!" To make matters worse, she discovered her open palm was on its way to making contact with his cheek.

She quickly pulled back, horrified by what she'd almost done—in full view of half the town no less. Several of her male cousins and her uncle rushed to her side.

As calmly as she could, she assured them she was fine. One of her cousins started past her, heading for Rorke with fists clenched and fire in his eyes. She reached out and stopped him. "No." Pulling her shoulders back, she stood as straight as possible and faced Rorke. "I apologize for losing my temper, Mr. O'Neil. I was out of line."

"Apology accepted, Ms. Harrison." He turned and walked toward his motorcycle. "I'll see you back at the house, Alex," he added over his shoulder.

Callie's throat tightened until she could barely breathe. Ten years ago when he'd walked away, she'd been fine since she'd expected to see him the next morning. Now she didn't know when, or even if, she'd ever see him again. Could she face the rest of her life never seeing him? Part of her longed to call out for him to stop, to let her feet move forward, until she was in his arms. But she'd just lost complete control of herself again—she had never lashed out like that before.

She knew what she had to do. She had to let him walk away.

Callie knocked on the door of her father's office at Harrison Manor. She'd already taken her suitcase upstairs and changed out of her maid of honor gown into a skirt and blouse. When there was no answer to her knock, she opened the door and peeked in. "Dad?"

Chandler Harrison looked up from the papers he was studying. "Calista, come in. I didn't hear you arrive."

She walked into his office. Hanging on the walls alongside his legitimate artwork were some of the paintings and drawings she'd done in high school.

"I can't believe you kept these."

He shrugged. "Are you hungry? I can have Nan fix something for you."

Apparently, his brief show of sentimental emotion at the end of their last meeting was all she was going to get. Although he didn't say anything, she knew the pictures' presence was her father's way of showing his pride in her. "No, thanks, I ate at the reception."

"How was the wedding?"

"Very nice."

"So, are you going back to New York tomorrow?"

"Yes, it's back to work bright and early Monday morning."

"From what I've been hearing, I'd expected you to decide to stay and marry O'Neil."

Callie was surprised her father seemed so calm about the possibility. She looked away. "For a moment I thought I might, too."

"I...uh..." He cleared his throat. "I hope you aren't letting anything I may have said in the past influence your decision."

"No."

"You know, I was only doing what I thought was in your best interest."

"I know."

"It wasn't always easy being a single parent."

"Dad, why did you lie to Rorke about why I'd left?" It didn't matter now, but she was curious.

"I knew he would try to find out where you'd gone. I assumed you'd stay in touch with your friends and sooner or later he'd have found out from someone where you were. But I also knew he wouldn't try if he thought you'd left him for money."

"It worked. Everything worked just the way you wanted."

"No, ultimately it backfired and I lost you." He folded his hands tightly together and leaned forward. "Calista, I never wanted to disown you. I thought the threat of it would bring you home. When it didn't, I hoped if I followed through and your grandmother told you what I'd done that would bring you running home to protest. But as we both know, it didn't work. Once the deed was done, I couldn't change it back. Harrison pride."

"Harrisons don't have the monopoly on pride in this town. Rorke's pride took a real beating when he thought I'd left him for money."

"I thought I was acting in your best interest. But then again, if I hadn't lied, he might not have gone on to be as successful as he is."

Callie was surprised by her father's words. "You know about Yankee?"

"I looked into the company as soon as they started looking at land around Harrison."

No wonder he'd been so unruffled about the possibility of her marrying Rorke. "Have you told anyone else?"

"I didn't think it was my place. People will know soon enough and then everyone in town will be saying they were his best friend way back when and how they always knew he would succeed. And the sad part is that they'll really believe it."

And fathers who had flown into a rage at the prospect of their daughters marrying him would graciously accept him as a son-in-law.

"After all the years they spent treating him like a second-class citizen?"

Her father nodded. "Money does strange things to some people. When you're a young man with a lot of it, you never know if a woman likes you for yourself or for your money. It meant a great deal to me that I met your mother, fell in love and had her accept my proposal of marriage before she knew I was rich."

Callie caught her bottom lip between her teeth. Could Rorke have been keeping the truth from her because he was afraid she would want him for his money and not because she still loved him? Especially after he found out her father had disowned her. "That's what started our argument. He didn't tell me about Yankee Motorworks being his."

"He may have needed to be sure it was him you wanted and not his money. Or he may not have known how to tell you. It's not something you blurt out to someone without sounding conceited. Did you ask him what he was doing these days?"

"I saw him working at the garage, so I assumed that was where he was working. When I asked what he'd been doing before coming back to Harrison, he said he'd been working on motorcycles."

"Well . . . he has been."

"He could have been more specific."

"But what was the status of your relationship at that point?"

"He still thought I'd left him for money."

He rubbed his temples. "I'm sorry."

"Dad, it's not your fault. You did what you thought was best for me. If you'd handled it differently, Yankee Motorworks might never have come into being."

"My personal contribution to strengthening American economics. But what have I cost you in the process and what have I cost Rorke?" He stood and walked around to the front of his desk, leaning against it. "I know you spent the night with him. And I know life's different in the big city, but I also know you and your moral upbringing and I'm sure you were with him only because you still have deep feelings for him."

She nodded. "Yes, I do."

"What are you going to do about it?"

Callie shrugged. "I've got a lot of thinking to do before I make a decision. Would you mind if I went for a drive?"

"When will you be back?"

"I'm not sure, but I'll be back before I head home. After all, my suitcase is upstairs."

"Are you going to see him?"

"I don't know."

Rorke and Jesse were playing pool in the den, when Alex walked in.

"Are you ready to go, Jesse?"

"Whenever you are," Jesse said. Although he continued to sink one ball after another into the pool table pockets, making no move to leave.

Rorke looked over at Alex. "Sure you guys don't want to stay another night?"

Alex shook his head. "No, thanks. I want to get back in enough time to unwind before getting ready for another work week."

Jesse laughed. "Couldn't be because there are fewer cars on the road at night to endanger your beloved Ferarri." There was a clicking noise as he made another perfect shot.

"That, too," Alex admitted. "Besides, I've got a feeling Rorke has some unfinished business to take care of tonight. Am I right, O'Neil?"

"I'd like to get into this game so I can try out my new pool table before Jesse wears out the felt."

Jesse looked up. "I think Alex was referring to the blonde?"

"Exactly." Alex sat down in a chair. "What's the story with Callie?"

"It's a long one."

Alex stretched out his legs and settled back. "Let's hear it."

Rorke sighed. "I thought you were in a hurry to leave."

"I wouldn't miss this for first shot at your little black book."

"Me, either." Jesse sunk the eight ball, returned his pool cue to the rack and took a seat on the couch.

Rorke put his own cue away. Then walked back and leaned against the table. He gave Alex and Jesse a watered-down version of his relationship with Callie, but in his mind he ran through it all. Starting with the night she'd had her flat tire.

She'd been so formal in her request for help, so polite, so proper. The only thing to suggest she saw him as anything more than someone she was paying for business services was the look of innocent wonder she'd had on her face as she'd climbed off the back of his motorcycle.

The moment had passed quickly and she was once more polite and proper. The same thing the afternoon she'd come by to pick up her repaired tire.

He'd been shocked when she'd come by again the next afternoon just to visit him. He could see how afraid of him she was.

She'd been afraid, but she'd felt something else and overcome her fears to pursue it. She would have pursued it all the way to the altar, facing up to possible ostracism from the town, if her father hadn't stepped in with his threats.

His rundown of the last two weeks, for his partners, was even less detailed, but he got his point across.

Jesse gave a slow whistle. "It's going to take more than a smile and a bouquet of flowers to get you out of this one."

Alex sat forward in his chair. "For what it's worth, when I asked if she was available, her answer was no. And I don't think your remarks in the parking lot would have made her as angry as they did if she didn't still care."

Rorke had suspected as much; plus he'd seen tears in her eyes during his toast, and she'd let him kiss her while they were dancing, although she hadn't seemed too happy about it.

He probably shouldn't have baited her the way he had in the parking lot, but when he'd watched her dance with Alex, it had been a struggle to keep from going over and cutting in. He knew she was hurting and vulnerable, easy prey for a smooth talker. And Alex was good—he'd taught him himself. He and Jesse had taken the shy business student with the black frame glasses and plastic pencil protector in his pocket and created a lady killer.

At first he'd thought he wanted to protect Callie, but then he realized what he was feeling was jealousy. It hurt him to think of her with another man.

"So, what are you going to do about it, O'Neil?" Alex broke into his thoughts.

"I could get roaring, mind-numbing drunk."

"Once the hangover clears, you'll be right back where you are now," Jesse said.

"True." Steve and Rachel had left for their honeymoon. Was Callie alone at Rachel's? "Maybe I'll take the Indian out for a spin."

Jesse stood and stretched. "I'm ready to go, Alex." He walked over to Rorke, clasped his shoulder in a gesture of support, then headed for the door.

After seeing them off, Rorke headed for the garage.

When he got to Rachel's, the house was dark and locked. Surely Callie wouldn't have left for New York already? It wouldn't be a safe trip for a woman alone at night. Could she be staying with family?

He drove slowly through town, then turned and headed back the way he'd come.

* * *

Callie had driven as far as the covered bridge over Harrison River before turning around and heading back. So many thoughts were tumbling around in her mind. The words of Rorke's toast to Steve and Rachel; Miss Dunsworth's encouragement to pursue Rorke and her implications that she regretted a decision she'd made earlier in her life, and the subtle warning that life alone wasn't paradise.

Mostly she was thinking about what her father had said about the difficulties of being wealthy.

In the near future everyone in Harrison would know about Rorke and Yankee—she suspected it would happen as soon as Miss Dunsworth remembered where she'd seen Alex and added that to his remark about working with Rorke.

Some of the old guard might still shun him—they could be a stubborn lot—but for the most part she imagined her father was right in predicting everyone would be claiming earlier friendship with Rorke. He would easily see right through them, turn within himself and be even more isolated than ever.

She wished she could be there for him.

Be there for him?

The phrase echoed through her thoughts. He needed her, just as he had ten years ago, and once again she was planning to run away and leave him.

Taking the next curve in the road, the Yankee billboard loomed along the side of the road. She pulled over, stopping about thirty feet in front of it. She got out of the car and stood looking up at the sign, lit by floodlights.

There he was—the stuff her dreams were made of— her knight in shining leather. And more importantly, the man she loved.

She thought back to the question that had entered her mind in church. If he'd told her about Yankee himself, would she have accepted it more easily? Making the discovery accidentally had knocked her off balance. It wasn't all a question of honesty and trust. Looking back she realized part of what she'd been feeling was hurt that he'd kept such a major part of his life secret from her.

The depths of her feelings were what had cracked the veneer of her social control...the manners and polite behavior she functioned by. If she stayed would she be able to take charge again? She wasn't sure, but she had to try. And hadn't she managed to stop herself from actually slapping him? Certainly, that was a good sign. Rorke was going to need her and she was determined to be there for him.

Her heart was beating wildly as she stood on his front porch and rang the doorbell. She was beginning to think no one was home, and then the door opened.

His hair was rumpled as though he'd been running his fingers through it. The tuxedo was gone, and all he wore was a pair of tight blue jeans that looked as if he'd had them for the past ten years. His expression was guarded. After her outburst at the church, maybe he didn't want her anymore.

Lifting her skirt to midthigh, she said, "I...um...I have this garter—"

Callie wasn't sure which one of them moved or whether they both moved, but she was in his arms, crushed tightly against his bare chest. His mouth coming down over hers cut off anything more she'd planned to say.

He still wanted her!

It was obvious from the way he was kissing her. A kiss full of passion. A kiss to unite her with him. A kiss of promises, asking nothing but love in return.

He pulled back, smiling down at her.

"Rorke, I'm so sorry."

He placed his finger over her lips. "Shh. It's all right. Everything's going to be all right." He stepped back and took her hand. After closing the front door, he led her into the living room. He sat down on the couch, pulling her into his lap.

She reached her arms around his neck and rested her head against his shoulder. His skin was warm against her cheek.

Rorke placed a soft kiss on her forehead. "Sweetheart, I'm sorry I didn't tell you about Yankee Motorworks."

"And I'm sorry I overreacted. It was such a shock. But the biggest problem wasn't that so much as the way I acted when I found out. Making a scene in front of all those people."

"It was a display of honest emotion, and sometimes when the emotions are very deep, people speak out spontaneously, rather than think first."

She leaned back to look up at him. "But I've never had that happen to me before and it frightened me. Frightened me so much, I was going to run away again. Despite what I said at the wedding about going through with my earlier plans, I was really running away."

"What made you change your mind?"

"A lot of things, but what it all boils down to is how very much I love you."

"I love you, too." He moved his lips over hers in a brief kiss. "And I want you to know I've never said those words to any other woman."

"Never? Not even in the time we were apart?"

"No. What other woman could compete with my golden-haired princess?"

She rested one hand on his cheek, moved forward to bring their mouths together. Once again, Rorke was the first to pull back. "So what do you say, Ms. Harrison? Shall we get married."

Trailing her fingers through the dark curls on his chest, she smiled up at him, her love shining in her eyes. "Yes, Mr. O'Neil, I think we should get married."

"Any preferences as to where or when?"

Callie shook her head. "Anywhere... anytime."

"You're easy to please," he teased.

"Not really. It's just the place and time are not nearly as important to me as who."

"We could get married in New York," he suggested.

"We could get married here in Harrison."

"St. Paul's?"

"What about in the meadow?" In the same place where they'd made vows in their hearts, they could make them out loud before the whole town.

"Anywhere you'd like."

Callie laughed. "Now who's being easy to please?"

"Frankly, I was surprised to hear you were still single."

"I won't be much longer."

Rorke smiled. "No, you won't be." He hugged her close. "I went to Rachel's earlier looking for you."

"I was at Harrison Manor."

"You've reconciled with your father?"

"'Reconciled' sounds more dramatic than what really happened. I went by there after I left here on Friday. He came home for lunch and it's been more or less business as usual since then, almost as though the last ten years hadn't happened."

"How do you think he'll take the news that we're going to get married?"

"He'll be fine." She sat up straighter so she could see him more clearly. "He already knew about you and Yankee."

"I'm surprised he didn't try to block the plant coming in."

"He's mellowed, Rorke. I think he has a lot of regrets."

"Don't we all?"

"Yes, but I'll never regret loving you . . . then, now or always."

"I intend to hold you to that promise." He placed his hand on her knee, then slowly moved it upward. "Now, about that garter . . ."

* * * * *

▼ SILHOUETTE

Desire

COMING NEXT MONTH

A NUISANCE
Lass Small

Man of the Month

Stefan Szyzsko was allergic to marriage-minded women but Carrie Pierce was about to change all that, despite the fact that Stefan had already dated and discarded her!

BRANIGAN'S BREAK
Leslie Davis Guccione

The latest novel in the Branigan Brothers series.

Sean Branigan was the struggling single father of two teenage daughters, but he resented Julia Hollins' attempts to advise him. She wasn't going to rearrange his family's life!

CHANCE AT A LIFETIME
Anne Marie Winston

Carrie Bradford couldn't bear to leave her husband, Ben, or their young daughter but her body had been destroyed. Perhaps there was another way to remain with them?

COMING NEXT MONTH

INTERRUPTED HONEYMOON
Modean Moon

After years of searching, Zack Gordon had finally found his wife, Barbara, but she was a stranger now—a stranger with a daughter...his daughter?

MIRACLE BABY
Shawna Delacorte

Rance Coulter was leery of women and children. Of course, that didn't stop him becoming passionately entangled with Darvi Stanton, but he wasn't going to be trapped into marriage!

PERIL IN PARADISE
Diana Mars

Investigative reporter Preston Kirkpatrick hated tropical islands, but he was determined to capture criminals and protect his uncle...until Clementine Cahill distracted him.

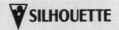

SILHOUETTE

SPECIAL EDITION

brings you...

A set of three linked titles every other month by Andrea Edwards

In June, don't miss A RING AND A PROMISE.
Montana rancher Jake MacNeill didn't know why he'd
impulsively come to Chicago but, once he'd set eyes on
Kate Mallory, he knew he wasn't going home without her!
Could an unfulfilled promise and an ancestral passion pledged
with a ring really influence these two modern lovers?

Look out for the next novel,
A ROSE AND A WEDDING VOW in August 1995,
when two *old* friends decide that love is worth taking a chance.

The trilogy concludes in October 1995 with
A SECRET AND A BRIDAL PLEDGE. Make sure
you get your copy!

THIS TIME, FOREVER—sometimes a love is
so strong, nothing can stand in its way...
not even time.

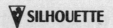

SILHOUETTE

> **SPECIAL EDITION** <

HOMETOWN HEARTBREAKERS:

These heart–stopping hunks are rugged, ready and able to steal your heart...

Silhouette Special Edition are proud to announce a new set of linked books from popular writer Susan Mallery.

Look out for:

THE BEST BRIDE – June 1995

Sexy Travis Haynes had a reputation as a lady–killer—until he rescued Elizabeth Abbott and gave her young daughter a temporary home. Who would have guessed that the rough, tough lawman had a softer side? It made Travis very tempting...

MARRIAGE ON DEMAND – July 1995

The women of Glenwood all agreed, Austin Lucas was as dangerous and desirable as any forbidden sin. But when an impulsive encounter obliged Rebecca Chambers to marry him, Rebecca wasn't sure their passion could lead to everlasting love.

COMING NEXT MONTH FROM

 **SILHOUETTE**

Sensation

*A thrilling mix of passion, adventure
and drama*

ONE LAST CHANCE Justine Davis
A SOLDIER'S HEART Kathleen Korbel
MISTRESS OF MAGIC Heather Graham Pozzessere
TWO AGAINST THE WORLD Mary Anne Wilson

Intrigue

*Danger, deception and desire—
new from Silhouette...*

ONLY SKIN DEEP Rebecca York
WHO IS JANE WILLIAMS? M.J. Rodgers
IN THEIR FOOTSTEPS Tess Gerritsen
WITHIN THE LAW Laraine McDaniel

Special Edition

Satisfying romances packed with emotion

HUSBAND: SOME ASSEMBLY REQUIRED
Marie Ferrarella
A RING AND A PROMISE Andrea Edwards
THE BEST BRIDE Susan Mallery
THE ADVENTURER Diana Whitney
A BED OF ROSES Elyn Day
WILD WINGS, WILD HEART Elizabeth Lane

SPRING FLOWERS COMPETITION

How would you like a years supply of Silhouette Special Editions ABSOLUTELY FREE? Well, you can win them all! All you have to do is complete the word puzzle below and send it in to us by 31st November 1995. The first 5 correct entries picked out of the bag after that date will win a years supply of Silhouette Special Editions (*six books every month - worth over £150*). What could be easier?

COWSLIP									
	L	L	E	B	E	U	L	B	Q
BLUEBELL	P	R	I	M	R	O	S	E	A
PRIMROSE	I	D	O	D	Y	U	I	P	R
DAFFODIL	L	O	X	G	O	R	S	E	Y
ANEMONE	S	T	H	R	I	F	T	M	S
DAISY	W	P	I	L	U	T	F	K	I
GORSE	O	E	N	O	M	E	N	A	A
TULIP	C	H	O	N	E	S	T	Y	D
HONESTY									
THRIFT									

PLEASE TURN OVER FOR DETAILS OF HOW TO ENTER

HOW TO ENTER

Hidden in the grid are various British flowers that bloom in the Spring. You'll find the list next to the word puzzle overleaf and they can be read backwards, forwards, up, down, or diagonally. When you find a word, circle it or put a line through it.

After you have completed your word search, don't forget to fill in your name and address in the space provided and pop this page in an envelope (you don't need a stamp) and post it today. Hurry - competition ends 31st November 1995.

Silhouette Spring Flower Competition,
FREEPOST,
P.O. Box 344,
Croydon,
Surrey. CR9 9EL

Are you a Reader Service Subscriber?   Yes ❑   No ❑

Ms/Mrs/Miss/Mr _____

Address _____

_____

_____ Postcode _____

One application per household.

You may be mailed with other offers from other reputable companies as a result of this application. If you would prefer not to receive such offers, please tick box. ❑

COMP195